DOVER · THRIFT · EDITIONS

The Eternal Husband

FYODOR DOSTOYEVSKY

Translated by
Constance Garnett

DOVER PUBLICATIONS, INC.
Mineola, New York

DOVER THRIFT EDITIONS

GENERAL EDITOR: MARY CAROLYN WALDREP
EDITOR OF THIS VOLUME: LISA PERNICIARO

Bibliographical Note

This Dover edition, first published in 2008, is an unabridged republication of the
Constance Garnett translation of the work, as originally published in the collection
The Eternal Husband and Other Stories by W. Heinemann, London, in 1917. A new
introductory Note has been specially prepared for this edition.

Library of Congress Cataloging-in-Publication Data

Dostoyevsky, Fyodor, 1821–1881.
    [Vechnyi muzh. English]
    The eternal husband / Fyodor Dostoyevsky ; translated by Constance Garnett.
      p. cm.
    "This Dover edition, first published in 2008, is an unabridged republication of the
Constance Garnett translation of the work, as originally published in the collection
The Eternal Husband and Other Stories by W. Heinemann, London, in 1917."
    ISBN-13: 978-0-486-46572-2
    ISBN-10: 0-486-46572-1
    I Garnett, Constance Black, 1862–1946. II. Title.

PG3326.V513 2008
891.73'3—dc22

                                      2007035681

Manufactured in the United States of America
Dover Publications, Inc., 31 East 2nd Street, Mineola, N.Y. 11501

Note

ALTHOUGH HIS reputation rests mainly on the longer works of his later years, many regard Dostoyevsky as master of the novella. *The Eternal Husband* may be his most perfect work in this genre.

Like his longer novels, *The Eternal Husband* has the psychological power and depth to draw the reader into the story and the characters. The reader will be ". . . drawn in, whirled round, blinded, suffocated, and at the same time filled with a giddy rapture," promised Virginia Woolf in her essay, *The Russian Point of View.*

The Eternal Husband is also a highly entertaining tale with a stunning conclusion, which makes it an excellent starting point for those new to Dostoyevsky.

Contents

1. VELCHANINOV

The summer had come and, contrary to expectations, Velchaninov remained in Petersburg. The trip he had planned to the south of Russia had fallen through, and the end of his case was not in sight. This case—a lawsuit concerning an estate—had taken a very unfortunate turn. Three months earlier it had appeared to be quite straightforward, almost impossible to contest; but suddenly everything was changed. "And, in fact, everything has changed for the worse!" Velchaninov began frequently and resentfully repeating that phrase to himself. He was employing an adroit, expensive, and distinguished lawyer, and was not sparing money; but through impatience and lack of confidence he had been tempted to meddle in the case himself too. He read documents and wrote statements which the lawyer rejected point-blank, ran from one court to another, collected evidence, and probably hindered everything; the lawyer complained, at any rate, and tried to pack him off to a summer villa. But Velchaninov could not even make up his mind to go away. The dust, the stifling heat, the white nights of Petersburg, that always fret the nerves were what he was enjoying in town. His flat was near the Grand Theatre; he had only recently taken it, and it, too, was a failure. "Everything is a failure!" he thought. His nervousness increased every day; but he had for a long time past been subject to nervousness and hypochondria.

He was a man whose life had been full and varied, he was by no means young, thirty-eight or even thirty-nine, and his "old age," as he expressed it himself, had come upon him "quite unexpectedly"; but he realized himself that he had grown older less by the number than by the quality, so to say, of his years, and that if he had begun to be aware of waning powers, the change was rather from within than from without. In appearance he was still strong and hearty. He was a tall, sturdily-built fellow, with thick flaxen hair without a sign of greyness and a long fair beard almost half-way down his chest; at first sight he seemed somewhat slack and clumsy, but if you looked more atten-

tively, you would detect at once that he was a man of excellent breed-
ing, who had at some time received the education of an aristocrat.
Velchaninov's manners were still free, assured and even gracious, in
spite of his acquired grumpiness and slackness. And he was still, even
now, full of the most unhesitating, the most snobbishly insolent self-
confidence, the depth of which he did not himself suspect, although
he was a man not merely intelligent, but even sometimes sensible, almost cultured and unmistakably gifted. His open and ruddy face had
been in old days marked by a feminine softness of complexion which
attracted the notice of women; and even now some people, looking at
him, would say: "What a picture of health! What a complexion!"
And yet this picture of health was cruelly subject to nervous depression. His eyes were large and blue, ten years earlier they had possessed
great fascination; they were so bright, so gay, so careless that they could
not but attract every one who came in contact with him. Now that
he was verging on the forties, the brightness and good-humour were
almost extinguished. Those eyes, which were already surrounded by
tiny wrinkles, had begun to betray the cynicism of a worn-out man
of doubtful morals, a duplicity, an ever-increasing irony and another
shade of feeling, which was new: a shade of sadness and of pain—a
sort of absent-minded sadness as though about nothing in particular
and yet acute. This sadness was especially marked when he was alone.
And, strange to say, this man who had been only a couple of years before fond of noisy gaiety, careless and good-humoured, who had been
so capital a teller of funny stories, liked nothing now so well as being
absolutely alone. He purposely gave up a great number of acquaintances whom he need not have given up even now, in spite of his fi-
nancial difficulties. It is true that his vanity counted for something in
this. With his vanity and mistrustfulness he could not have endured
the society of his old acquaintances. But, by degrees, in solitude even
his vanity began to change its character. It grew no less, quite the contrary, indeed; but it began to develop into a special sort of vanity
which was new in him; it began at times to suffer from different
causes—from unexpected causes which would have formerly been
quite inconceivable, from causes of a "higher order" than ever before—"if one may use such an expression, if there really are higher or
lower causes. . . ." This he added on his own account.

Yes, he had even come to that; he was worrying about some sort of
higher ideas of which he would never have thought twice in earlier
days. In his own mind and in his conscience he called "higher" all
"ideas" at which (he found to his surprise) he could not laugh in his
heart—there had never been such hitherto—in his secret heart only,
of course; oh, in company it was a different matter! He knew very

well, indeed, that—if only the occasion were to arise—he would the very next day, in spite of all the mysterious and reverent resolutions of his conscience, with perfect composure disavow all these "higher ideas" and be the first to turn them into ridicule, without, of course, admitting anything. And this was really the case, in spite of a certain and, indeed, considerable independence of thought, which he had of late gained at the expense of the "lower ideas" that had mastered him till then. And how often, when he got up in the morning, he began to be ashamed of the thoughts and feelings he had passed through during a sleepless night! And he had suffered continually of late from sleeplessness. He had noticed for some time past that he had become excessively sensitive about everything, trifles as well as matters of importance, and so he made up his mind to trust his feelings as little as possible. But he could not overlook some facts, the reality of which he was forced to admit. Of late his thoughts and sensations were sometimes at night completely transformed, and for the most part utterly unlike those which came to him in the early part of the day. This struck him—and he even consulted a distinguished doctor who was, however, an acquaintance; he spoke to him about it jocosely, of course. The answer he received was that the transformation of ideas and sensations, and even the possession of two distinct sets of thoughts and sensations, was a universal fact among persons "who think and feel," that the convictions of a whole lifetime were sometimes transformed under the melancholy influences of night and sleeplessness; without rhyme or reason most momentous decisions were taken; but all this, of course, was only true up to a certain point—and, in fact, if the subject were too conscious of the double nature of his feelings, so that it began to be a source of suffering to him, it was certainly a symptom of approaching illness; and then steps must be taken at once. The best thing of all was to make a radical change in the mode of life, to alter one's diet, or even to travel. Relaxing medicine was beneficial, of course.

Velchaninov did not care to hear more; but to his mind it was conclusively shown to be illness.

"And so all this is only illness, all these 'higher ideas' are mere illness and nothing more!" he sometimes exclaimed to himself resentfully. He was very loth to admit this.

Soon, however, what had happened exclusively in the hours of the night began to be repeated in the morning, only with more bitterness than at night, with anger instead of remorse, with irony instead of emotion. What really happened was that certain incidents in his past, even in his distant past, began suddenly, and God knows why, to come more and more frequently back to his mind, but they came back in quite a peculiar way. Velchaninov had, for instance, complained for a long time past of loss of memory: he would forget the faces of acquaintances, who were offended by his cutting them when they met; he sometimes completely forgot a book he had read months before; and yet in spite of this loss of memory, evident every day (and a source of great uneasiness to him), everything concerning the remote past, things that had been quite forgotten for ten or fifteen years, would sometimes come suddenly into his mind now with such amazing exactitude of details and impressions that he felt as though he were living through them again. Some of the facts he remembered had been so completely forgotten that it seemed to him a miracle that they could be recalled. But this was not all, and, indeed, what man of wide experience has not some memory of a peculiar sort? But the point was that all that was recalled came back now with a quite fresh, surprising and, till then, inconceivable point of view, and seemed as though some one were leading up to it on purpose. Why did some things he remembered strike him now as positive crimes? And it was not a question of the judgments of his mind only: he would have put little faith in his gloomy, solitary and sick mind; but it reached the point of curses and almost of tears, of inward tears. Why, two years before, he would not have believed it if he had been told that he would ever shed tears! At first, however, what he remembered was rather of a mortifying than of a sentimental character: he recalled certain failures and humiliations in society; he remembered, for instance, how he had been slandered by an intriguing fellow, and in consequence refused admittance to a certain house; how, for instance, and not so long ago, he had been publicly and unmistakably insulted, and had not challenged the offender to a duel; how in a circle of very pretty women he had been made the subject of an extremely witty epigram and had found no suitable answer. He even recollected one or two unpaid debts—trifling ones, it is true, but debts of honour—owing to people whom he had given up visiting and even spoke ill of. He was also worried (but only in his worst moments) by the thought of the two fortunes, both considerable ones, which he had squandered in the stupidest way possible. But soon he began to remember things of a "higher order."

Suddenly, for instance, apropos of nothing, he remembered the forgotten, utterly forgotten, figure of a harmless, grey-headed and absurd old clerk, whom he had once, long, long ago, and with absolute impunity, insulted in public simply to gratify his own conceit, simply for the sake of an amusing and successful jest, which was repeated and increased his prestige. The incident had been so completely forgotten that he could not even recall the old man's surname, though all the surroundings of the incident rose before his mind with incredible clearness. He distinctly remembered that the old man was defending his daughter, who was unmarried, though no longer quite young, and had become the subject of gossip in the town. The old man had begun to answer angrily, but he suddenly burst out crying before the whole company, which made some sensation. They had ended by making him drunk with champagne as a joke and getting a hearty laugh out of it. And now when, apropos of nothing, Velchaninov remembered how the poor old man had sobbed and hidden his face in his hands like a child, it suddenly seemed to him as though he had never forgotten it. And, strange to say, it had all seemed to him very amusing at the time, especially some of the details, such as the way he had covered his face with his hands; but now it was quite the contrary.

Later, he recalled how, simply as a joke, he had slandered the very pretty wife of a schoolmaster, and how the slander had reached the husband's ears. Velchaninov had left the town soon after and never knew what the final consequences of his slander had been, but now he began to imagine how all might have ended—and there is no knowing to what lengths his imagination might not have gone if this memory had not suddenly been succeeded by a much more recent reminiscence of a young girl of the working-class, to whom he had not even felt attracted, and of whom, it must be admitted, he was actually ashamed. Yet, though he could not have said what had induced him, he had got her into trouble and had simply abandoned her and his child without even saying good-bye (it was true, he had no time to spare), when he left Petersburg. He had tried to find that girl for a whole year afterwards, but he had not succeeded in tracing her. He had, it seemed, hundreds of such reminiscences—and each one of them seemed to bring dozens of others in its train. By degrees his vanity, too, began to suffer.

We have said already that his vanity had degenerated into something peculiar. That was true. At moments (rare moments, however), he even forgot himself to such a degree that he ceased to be ashamed of not keeping his own carriage, that he trudged on foot from one court to another, that he began to be somewhat negligent in his dress. And if some one of his own acquaintance had scanned him with a sarcastic stare in the street or had simply refused to recognize him, he might really have had pride enough to pass him by without a frown. His indifference would have been genuine, not assumed for effect. Of course, this was only at times: these were only the moments of forgetfulness and nervous irritation, yet his vanity had by degrees grown less concerned with the subjects that had once affected it, and was becoming concentrated on one question, which haunted him continually.

"Why, one would think," he began reflecting satirically sometimes (and he almost always began by being satirical when he thought about himself), "why, one would think some one up aloft were anxious for the reformation of my morals, and were sending me these cursed reminiscences and 'tears of repentance'! So be it, but it's all useless! It is all shooting with blank cartridges! As though I did not know for certain, more certainly than certainty, that in spite of these fits of tearful remorse and self-reproach, I haven't a grain of independence for all my foolish middle age! Why, if the same temptation were to turn up to-morrow, if circumstances, for instance, were to make it to my interest to spread a rumour that the schoolmaster's wife had taken presents from me, I should certainly spread it, I shouldn't hesitate—and it would be even worse, more loathsome than the first time, just because it would be the second time and not the first time. Yes, if I were insulted again this minute by that little prince whose leg I shot off eleven years ago, though he was the only son of his mother, I should challenge him at once and condemn him to crutches again. So they are no better than blank cartridges, and there's no sense in them! And what's the good of remembering the past when I've not the slightest power of escaping from myself?"

And though the adventure with the schoolmaster's wife was not repeated, though he did not condemn any one else to crutches, the very idea that it inevitably would be the same, if the same circumstances arose, almost killed him . . . at times. One cannot, in reality, suffer from memories all the time; one can rest and enjoy oneself in the intervals.

So, indeed, Velchaninov did: he was ready to enjoy himself in the intervals; yet his sojourn in Petersburg grew more and more unpleasant as time went on. July was approaching. Intermittently he had flashes of determination to give up everything, the lawsuit and all, and to go away somewhere without looking back, to go suddenly, on the spur of the moment, to the Crimea, for instance. But, as a rule, an hour later he had scorned the idea and had laughed at it: "These hateful thoughts won't stop short at sending me to the south, if once they've begun and if I've any sense of decency, and so it's useless to run away from them, and, indeed, there's no reason to.

"And what's the object of running away?" he went on brooding in his despondency; "it's so dusty here, so stifling, everything in the house is so messy. In those lawcourts where I hang about among those busy people, there is such a scurrying to and fro like mice, such a mass of sordid cares! All the people left in town, all the faces that flit by from morning till night so naïvely and openly betray their self-love, their guileless insolence, the cowardice of their little souls, the chicken-heartedness of their little natures—why, it's a paradise for a melancholy man, seriously speaking! Everything is open, everything is clear, no one thinks it necessary to hide anything as they do among our gentry in our summer villas or at watering-places abroad—and so it's more deserving of respect, if only for its openness and simplicity! . . . I won't go away! I'll stay here if I burst!"

2. THE GENTLEMAN WITH CRAPE ON HIS HAT

It was the third of July. The heat and stuffiness were insufferable. The day had been a very busy one for Velchaninov; he had had to spend the whole morning in walking and driving from place to place, and he had before him the prospect of an unavoidable visit that evening to a gentleman—a lawyer and a civil councillor—whom he hoped to catch unawares at his villa out of town. At six o'clock Velchaninov went at last into a restaurant (the fare was not beyond criticism, though the cooking was French) on the Nevsky Prospect, near the Police Bridge. He sat down at the little table in his usual corner and asked for the dinner of the day.

He used to eat the dinner that was provided for a rouble and paid extra for the wine, and he regarded this as a sacrifice to the unsettled state of his finances and an act of prudence on his part. Though he wondered how he could possibly eat such stuff, he nevertheless used to devour it to the last crumb—and every time with as much appetite as though he had not eaten for three days before. "There's something morbid about it," he would mutter to himself sometimes, noticing his appetite. But on this occasion he took his seat at his little table in a very bad humour, tossed his hat down angrily, put his elbows on the table, and sank into thought.

Though he could be so polite and, on occasion, so loftily imperturbable, he would probably now, if some one dining near him had been noisy, or the boy waiting on him had failed to understand at the first word, have been as blustering as a *junker* and would perhaps have made a scene.

The soup was put before him. He took up the ladle, but before he had time to help himself, he dropped it, and almost jumped up from the table. A surprising idea suddenly dawned upon him: at that instant—and God knows by what process—he suddenly realized the cause of his depression, of the special extra depression which had tormented him of late for several days together, had for some unknown reason fastened upon him and for some unknown cause refused to be shaken off; now he suddenly saw it all and it was as plain as a pikestaff.

"It's all that hat," he muttered as though inspired. "It's nothing but that cursed bowler hat with that beastly mourning crape that is the cause of it all!"

He began pondering—and the more he pondered the more morose he grew, and the more extraordinary "the whole adventure" seemed to him.

"But . . . it is not an adventure, though," he protested, distrustful of himself. "As though there were anything in the least like an adventure about it!"

All that had happened was this. Nearly a fortnight before (he did not really remember, but he fancied it was about a fortnight), he had first met somewhere in the street, near the corner of Podyatchesky Street and Myestchansky Street, a gentleman with crape on his hat. The gentleman was like any one else, there was nothing peculiar about him, he passed quickly, but he stared somewhat too fixedly at Velchaninov, and for some reason at once attracted his attention in a marked degree. His countenance struck Velchaninov as familiar. He had certainly at some time met it somewhere. "But I must have seen thousands of faces in my life, I can't remember them all!"

Before he had gone twenty paces further he seemed to have forgotten the encounter, in spite of the impression made at first. But the impression persisted the whole day—and it was somewhat singular, it took the form of a peculiar undefined annoyance. Now, a fortnight later, he remembered all that distinctly; he remembered, too, what he had failed to grasp at the time—that is, what his annoyance was due to; and he had so utterly failed to grasp it that he had not even connected his ill-humour all that evening with the meeting that morning.

But the gentleman had lost no time in recalling himself to Velchaninov's mind, and next day had come across the latter in the Nevsky Prospect again, and again stared at him rather strangely. Velchaninov dismissed him with a curse and immediately afterwards wondered why he cursed. It is true that there are faces that at once arouse an undefined and aimless aversion.

"Yes, I certainly have met him somewhere," he muttered thoughtfully, an hour after the meeting. And he remained in a very bad humour the whole evening afterwards; he even had a bad dream at night, and yet it never entered his head that the whole cause of this new fit of despondency was nothing but that gentleman in mourning, although he did not once think of him that evening! He had even been wrathful at the moment that such a "wretched object" could occupy his attention as long as it did and would certainly have thought it degrading to ascribe his agitation to him, if it had ever occurred to his mind to do so. Two days later they met again in a crowd coming off one of the Nevsky steamers. On this third occasion Velchaninov was ready to swear that the gentleman with the crape on his hat recognized him and made a dash for him, but was borne away in the crush; he fancied he had even had the "effrontery" to hold out his hand to him; perhaps he had even cried out and shouted his name. That, however, Velchaninov had not heard distinctly, but . . . "Who is the low fellow, though, and why does he not come up to me, if he really does know me, and if he is so anxious to?" he thought angrily, as he got into a cab and drove towards Smolny monastery. Half-an-hour later he was noisily arguing with his lawyer, but in the evening and the night he was suffering again from the most abominable and most fantastic attack of acute depression. "Am I in for a bilious attack?" he wondered uneasily, looking at himself in the looking-glass.

This was the third meeting. Afterwards, for five days in succession, he met "no one," and not a sign was seen of the low fellow. And yet the gentleman with the crape on his hat was continually in his mind. With some surprise Velchaninov caught himself wondering: "What's the matter with me—am I sick on his account, or what? H'm! . . . and he must have a lot to do in Petersburg, too—and for whom is he wearing crape? He evidently recognized me, but I don't recognize him. And why do these people put on crape? It's out of keeping with him somehow. . . . I fancy if I look at him closer, I shall recognize him. . . ."

And something seemed faintly stirring in his memory, like some familiar but momentarily forgotten word, which one tries with all one's might to recall; one knows it very well and knows that one knows it; one knows exactly what it means, one is close upon it and yet it refuses to be remembered, in spite of one's efforts.

"It was . . . It was long ago . . . and it was somewhere . . . There was . . . there was . . . but, damn the fellow, whatever there was or wasn't. . . ." he cried angrily all at once; "it is not worth while to demean and degrade myself over that wretched fellow. . . ."

He grew horribly angry, but in the evening, when he suddenly remembered that he had been angry that morning, and "horribly" angry, it was extremely disagreeable to him; he felt as though some one had caught him in something shameful. He was bewildered and surprised.

"There there must be reason for my being so angry . . . apropos of nothing . . . at a mere reminiscence . . ." He left the thought unfinished.

And next day he felt angrier than ever, but this time he fancied he had grounds for it, and that he was quite right in feeling so; "It was unheard-of insolence," he thought. What had happened was the fourth meeting. The gentleman with crape on his hat had suddenly made his appearance again, as though he had sprung out of the earth. Velchaninov had just caught in the street the indispensable civil councillor before mentioned, of whom he was still in pursuit, meaning to pounce on him unawares at his summer villa, for the gentleman, whom Velchaninov scarcely knew, though it was so necessary to see him about his business, on that occasion as on this eluded him, and was evidently keeping out of sight and extremely reluctant to meet him. Delighted at coming across him at last, Velchaninov walked hurriedly beside him, glancing into his face and straining every effort to bring the wily old fellow to the discussion of a certain subject, in which the latter might be indiscreet enough to let slip the facts of which he had so long been on the track; but the crafty old man had his own views, and kept putting him off with laughter or silence—and it was just at this extremely absorbing moment that Velchaninov descried on the opposite pavement the gentleman with crape on his hat. He was standing staring at them both—he was watching them, that was evident, and seemed to be jeering at them.

"Damnation!" cried Velchaninov in a fury, as he left the civil councillor at his destination and ascribed his failure with him to the sudden appearance of that "impudent fellow." "Damnation! is he spying on me? He's evidently following me. Hired by some one, perhaps, and . . . and . . . and, by Jove! he was jeering at me! By Jove! I'll thrash him. . . . I'm sorry I've no stick with me! I'll buy a stick! I won't let it pass. Who is he? I insist on knowing who he is."

It was three days after this fourth meeting that Velchaninov was at his restaurant, as we have described him, agitated in earnest and even somewhat overwhelmed. He could not help being conscious of it himself, in spite of his pride. He was forced at last, putting all the circumstances together, to suspect that all his depression—all this *peculiar* despondency and the agitation that had persisted for the last fortnight—was caused by no other than this gentleman in mourning, "nonentity as he was."

"I may be a hypochondriac," thought Velchaninov, "and so I am ready to make a mountain out of a molehill, but does it make it any better for me that all this is *perhaps* only fancy! Why, if every rogue like that is going to be able to upset one in this way, why . . . it's . . . why? . . ."

Certainly in the meeting of that day (the fifth), which had so agitated Velchaninov, the mountain had proved to be little more than a mole-hill: the gentleman had as before darted by him, but this time without scrutinizing Velchaninov, and without, as before, betraying that he recognized him; on the contrary, he dropped his eyes and seemed to be very anxious to escape being noticed. Velchaninov turned round and shouted at the top of his voice—

"Hi! you with the crape on your hat! Hiding now! Stop! Who are you?"

The question (and his shouting altogether) was very irrational, but Velchaninov only realized that after he had uttered it. The gentleman turned round at the shout, stood still for a minute disconcerted, smiled, seemed on the point of doing or saying something, was obviously for a minute in a state of the utmost indecision, then he suddenly turned and rushed away without looking back. Velchaninov looked after him with astonishment.

"And what if it's a case of my forcing myself on him, not his forcing himself on me?" he thought. "And that's all it amounts to?"

When he had finished dinner he made haste to set off to the summer villa to see the civil councillor. He did not find him; he was informed that "his honour had not returned that day, and probably would not come back till three or four o'clock in the morning, as he was staying in town to a birthday party." This was so mortifying that, in his first fury, Velchaninov decided himself to go to the birthday party, and even set off to do so; but reflecting on the road that it was a long way to go, he dismissed the cab and trudged home on foot to his flat near the Grand Theatre. He felt that he wanted exercise. He must, at all costs, overcome his usual sleeplessness, and sleep sound that night, to soothe his excited nerves; and in order to sleep he must anyway be tired. And, as it was a long walk, it was half-past ten before he reached home, and he certainly was very tired.

Though he so criticized the flat that he had taken the previous March, and abused it so malignantly—excusing himself to himself on the plea that he was only "camping there temporarily," and stranded in Petersburg through that "damned lawsuit"—the flat was by no means so bad and so unsuitable as he made out. The approach was certainly rather dark and "grubby" under the gateway, but the flat itself, on the second storey, consisted of two big, lofty and bright rooms, separated from one another by a dark entry, and looking one into the street, the other into the courtyard. Adjoining the room the windows of which looked into the courtyard was a small study, which had been designed for a bedroom; but Velchaninov kept it littered with books and papers; he slept in one of the larger rooms, the one that looked into the street. He had a bed made up on the sofa. The furniture was quite decent, though second-hand, and he had besides a few articles of value—the relics of his former prosperity: bronze and china, and big, genuine Bokhara rugs; even two good pictures had been preserved; but everything had been unmistakably untidy and even dusty and nothing had been put in its place ever since his servant, Pelagea, had gone home to Novgorod for a holiday and left him alone. The oddity of having a solitary female servant for a bachelor and man of the world who was still anxious to keep up the style of a gentleman almost made Velchaninov blush, though he was very well satisfied with his Pelagea. The girl had come to him when he was taking the flat in the spring, from a family of his acquaintance who were going abroad, and she had put the flat to rights. But when she went away he could not bring himself to engage another woman; to engage a manservant was not worth while for a short time; besides, he did not like menservants. And so it was arranged that the sister of the porter's wife should come in every morning to clear up and that Velchaninov should leave the key at the porter's lodge when he went out. She did absolutely nothing, merely pocketed her wages; and he suspected her of pilfering. Yet he dismissed everything with a shrug and was positively glad that he was left quite alone in the flat. But there are limits to everything; and at some jaundiced moments the "filth" was absolutely insufferable to his nerves, and he almost always went into his rooms with a feeling of repugnance on returning home.

But this time he barely gave himself time to undress; flinging himself on the bed, he irritably resolved to think of nothing, but to go to sleep "this minute," whatever might happen; and, strange to say, he did fall asleep as soon as his head touched the pillow; such a thing had not happened to him for almost a month.

He slept for nearly three hours, but his sleep was uneasy, and he had strange dreams such as one has in fever. He dreamed of some crime which he had committed and concealed and of which he was accused by people who kept coming up to him. An immense crowd collected, but more people still came, so that the door was not shut but remained open. But his whole interest was centered on a strange person, once an intimate friend of his, who was dead, but now somehow suddenly came to see him. What made it most worrying was that Velchaninov did not know the man, had forgotten his name and could not recall it. All he knew was that he had once liked him very much. All the other people who had come up seemed expecting from this man a final word that would decide Velchaninov's guilt or innocence, and all were waiting impatiently. But he sat at the table without moving, was mute and would not speak. The noise did not cease for a moment, the general irritation grew more intense, and suddenly in a fury Velchaninov struck the man for refusing to speak, and felt a strange enjoyment in doing it. His heart thrilled with horror and misery at what he had done, but there was enjoyment in that thrill. Utterly exasperated, he struck him a second time and a third, and, drunk with rage and terror, which reached the pitch of madness, but in which there was an intense enjoyment, he lost count of his blows, and went on beating him without stopping. He wanted to demolish *it* all, all. Suddenly something happened: they all shrieked horribly and turned round to the door, as though expecting something, and at that instant there came the sound of a ring at the bell, repeated three times, with violence enough to pull the bell off. Velchaninov woke up and was wide-awake in an instant. He leapt headlong out of bed and rushed to the door; he was absolutely convinced that the ring at the bell was not a dream and that some one really had rung at his bell that moment. "It would be too unnatural for such a distinct, such a real, palpable ring to be only a dream!"

But to his surprise the ring at the bell turned out to be a dream, too. He opened the door, went out on the landing, even peeped down the stairs—there was absolutely no one there. The bell hung motionless. Surprised, but relieved, he went back into his room. When he had lighted a candle he remembered that he had left the door closed but not locked or bolted. He had sometimes in the past forgotten when he came home to lock the door for the night, not thinking it of much importance.

Pelagea had often given him a talking-to about it. He went back into the passage, shut the door, opened it once more and looked out on the landing, but only fastened the door on the inside with the hook, without taking the trouble to turn the key. The clock struck half-past two; so he must have slept three hours.

His dream had so disturbed him that he did not want to go to bed again at once, and made up his mind to walk up and down his room for half an hour or—"Time enough to smoke a cigar"—he thought. Hastily dressing, he went to the window and lifted the thick stuff curtain and the white blind behind it. It was already daylight in the street. The light summer nights of Petersburg always worked on his nerves and of late had intensified his insomnia, so that it was expressly on this account that he had, a fortnight previously, put up thick stuff curtains which completely excluded the light when they were fully drawn. Letting in the daylight and forgetting the lighted candle on the table, he fell to pacing up and down the room, still oppressed by a sort of sick and heavy feeling. The impression of the dream was still upon him. A real feeling of distress that he should have been capable of raising his hand against that man and beating him still persisted.

"That man doesn't exist, and never has existed; it's all a dream. Why am I worrying about it?"

He began thinking with exasperation, as though all his troubles were concentrated on this, that he was certainly beginning to be ill— "A sick man."

It was always painful to him to think that he was getting old and growing feebler, and in his bad moments he exaggerated his age and failing powers on purpose to irritate himself.

"Old age," he muttered; "I'm getting quite old, I'm losing my memory, I see apparitions, I dream dreams, bells ring. . . . Damn it all, I know from experience that such dreams are always a sign of fever with me. . . . I am convinced that all this business with the crape gentleman is a dream too. I was certainly right yesterday: it's I, I, who am pestering him, not he me. I've woven a romance about him, and I am hiding under the table in my fright at it. And why do I call him a low fellow? He may be a very decent person. His face is not attractive, certainly, though there is nothing particularly ugly about it; he's dressed like any one else. Only in his eyes there's something. . . . Here I'm at it again! I'm thinking about him again!! What the devil does the look in his eyes matter to me? Can't I get on without that? . . ."

Among the thoughts that kept starting up in his mind, one rankled painfully: he felt suddenly convinced that this gentleman with the crape on his hat had once been an acquaintance on friendly terms with him, and now sneered at him when he met him because he knew some great secret about him in the past and saw him now in such a humiliating position. He went mechanically to the window, meaning to open it and get a breath of the night air, and—and he suddenly shuddered all over: it seemed to him that something incredible and unheard-of was suddenly happening before his eyes.

He had not yet opened the window but he made haste to slip behind the corner of the window and hide himself: on the deserted pavement opposite he had suddenly seen directly facing the house the man with the crape on his hat. The gentleman was standing on the pavement looking towards his windows, but evidently not noticing him, stared inquisitively at the house as though considering something. He seemed to be deliberating and unable to decide: he lifted his hand and seemed to put his finger to his forehead. At last he made up his mind: he took a cursory glance round, and began stealthily on tiptoe crossing the street. Yes: he had gone in at the gateway by the little gate (which sometimes in summer was left unbolted till three o'clock).

"He's coming to me," flashed on Velchaninov's mind, and, also on tiptoe, he ran headlong to the door and stood before it silent and numb with suspense, softly laying his trembling right hand on the hook of the door he had just fastened, listening intently for the sound of footsteps on the stairs.

His heart beat so violently that he was afraid he might not hear the stranger come up on tiptoe. He did not understand what it meant, but he felt it all with tenfold intensity. His dream seemed to have melted into reality. Velchaninov was by temperament bold. He sometimes liked to display fearlessness in the face of danger even if he were only admiring himself with no one else to look at him. But now there was something else as well. The man who had so lately been given up to hypochondria and nervous depression was completely transformed; he was not the same man. A nervous, noiseless laugh broke from him. From behind the closed door he divined every movement of the stranger.

"Ah! now he's coming in, he has come in, he's looking about him; he's listening downstairs; he's holding his breath, stealing up . . . ah! He has taken hold of the handle, he's pulling it, trying it! He reckoned on its not being locked! So he knows I sometimes forget to lock it! He's pulling at the handle again; why, does he imagine that the hook will come out? It's a pity to part! Isn't it a pity to let him go like this?"

And indeed everything must have happened just as he pictured it; someone really was standing on the other side of the door, and was softly and noiselessly trying the lock, and was pulling at the handle and—"Of course, he had his object in doing so." But by now Velchaninov had resolved to settle the question, and with a sort of glee got ready for the moment. He had an irresistible longing to unfasten the hook, suddenly to fling open the door, and to confront the "bugbear" face to face. "What may you be doing here, pray, honoured sir?"

And so he did: seizing the moment, he suddenly lifted the hook, pushed the door and—almost fell over the gentleman with crape on his hat.

3. PAVEL PAVLOVITCH TRUSOTSKY

The latter stood speechless, rooted to the spot. They stood facing one another in the doorway, and stared fixedly into each other's faces. Some moments passed and suddenly—Velchaninov recognized his visitor!

At the same time the visitor evidently realized that Velchaninov recognized him fully. There was a gleam in his eye that betrayed it. In one instant his whole face melted into a sugary smile.

"I have the pleasure, I believe, of addressing Alexey Ivanovitch?" he almost chanted in a voice of deep feeling, ludicrously incongruous with the circumstances.

"Surely you are not Pavel Pavlovitch Trusotsky?" Velchaninov brought out with an air of perplexity.

"We were acquainted nine years ago at T——, and if you will allow me to remind you—we were intimately acquainted."

"Yes . . . to be sure, but now it's three o'clock, and for the last ten minutes you've been trying whether my door was locked or not."

"Three o'clock!" cried the visitor, taking out his watch and seeming positively grieved and surprised; "why, so it is. Three! I beg your pardon, Alexey Ivanovitch, I ought to have considered before coming up: I'm quite ashamed. I'll come again and explain, in a day or two, but now . . ."

"No! If there's to be an explanation will you kindly give it me this minute!" Velchaninov caught him up. "Please walk inside, into this room—no doubt you intended to come into the room yourself, and have not turned up in the middle of the night simply to try the lock."

He was excited and at the same time disconcerted, and felt that he could not grasp the position. He was even somewhat ashamed—there proved to be neither mystery nor danger. The whole phantasmagoria had proved to be nothing; all that had turned up was the foolish figure of some Pavel Pavlovitch. And yet he did not believe that it was all so simple; he had a vague presentiment and dread of something. Making his visitor sit down in an arm-chair, he seated himself impatiently on his bed, not a yard away, bent forward with his hands on his knees and waited irritably for him to speak. He scanned him greedily and remembered him. But, strange to say, the man was silent, quite silent, and seemed not to realize that he was "in duty bound" to speak at once; on the contrary, he, too, gazed at Velchaninov with a look of expectation. It was possible that he was simply timid, feeling at first a certain awkwardness like a mouse in a trap; but Velchaninov flew into a rage.

"What do you mean by it!" he cried; "you are not a phantom or a dream, I suppose! You've not come to play at being dead, surely? Explain yourself, my good man!"

The visitor fidgeted, smiled, and began warily—

"So far as I see, what strikes you most of all is my coming at such an hour and under such peculiar circumstances. . . . So that, remembering all the past, and how we parted—it's really strange to me now.... Though, indeed, I had no intention of calling, and it has only happened by accident...."

"How by accident? Why, I saw you through the window run across the street on tiptoe!"

"Ah, you saw me! So perhaps you know more about it all than I do! But I'm only irritating you.... You see, I arrived here three weeks ago on business of my own.... I am Pavel Pavlovitch Trusotsky, you know; you recognized me yourself. I am here to try to get transferred to another province, and to a post in another department considerably superior.... But all that's neither here nor there, though ... The point is, if you must know, that I have been hanging about here for the last three weeks, and I seem to be spinning out my business on purpose—that is, the business of my transfer—and really, if it comes off I do believe I shan't notice that it has come off and shall stay on in your Petersburg, feeling as I do now. I hang about as though I had lost sight of my object and, as it were, pleased to have lost sight of it—feeling as I do! ..."

"Feeling how?" Velchaninov asked, frowning.

The visitor raised his eyes to him, lifted his hat and pointed to the crape on it.

"Why, look; that's how I'm feeling."

Velchaninov gazed blankly first at the crape and then at the countenance of his visitor. Suddenly the colour rushed into his cheeks and he grew terribly agitated.

"Surely not Natalya Vassilyevna?"

"Yes! Natalya Vassilyevna! Last March ... consumption, and almost suddenly, after two or three months' illness! And I am left—as you see!"

As he said this the visitor, in deep emotion, put out his hands on each side, the hat with the crape on it flapping in his left one, while he made a low bow that displayed his bald head for ten seconds at least.

His air and his gesture seemed to revive Velchaninov; an ironical and even provocative smile hovered on his lips—but only for a moment: the news of the death of this lady (whom he had known so long ago and had long ago succeeded in forgetting) gave him a shock which was a complete surprise to him.

"Is it possible?"—he muttered the first words that came to his tongue—"and why didn't you come straight and tell me?"

"I thank you for your sympathy. I see it and appreciate it, in spite of ..."

"In spite of?"

"In spite of so many years of separation, you have just shown such sympathy for my sorrow and even for me that I am, of course, sensible of gratitude. That was all I wanted to express. It's not that I had doubts of my friends: I can find here the truest friends at once—Stepan Mihalovitch Bagautov, for instance. But you know, Alexey Ivanovitch, our acquaintance with you—friendship rather, as I gratefully recall it—was over nine years ago, you never came back to us; there was no interchange of letter. . . ."

The visitor chanted his phrases as though to music, but all the while that he was holding forth he looked at the floor, though, no doubt, all the time he saw everything. But Velchaninov had by now regained his composure.

With a very strange impression, which grew stronger and stronger, he listened to Pavel Pavlovitch and watched him, and when the latter suddenly paused, the most incongruous and surprising ideas rushed in a sudden flash into his mind.

"But how was it I didn't recognize you till now?" he cried, growing more animated. "Why, we've stumbled across each other five times in the street!"

"Yes; I remember that, too; you were constantly crossing my path—twice, or perhaps three times. . . ."

"That is, *you* were constantly coming upon me, not I upon you."

Velchaninov stood up and suddenly, quite unexpectedly, he began laughing. Pavel Pavlovitch paused, looked at him attentively, but at once continued—

"And as for your not recognizing me, you might well have forgotten me, and, besides, I've had smallpox and it has left some traces on my face."

"Smallpox? To be sure, he has had smallpox! However did you——"

"Manage that? Anything may happen. One never can tell, Alexey Ivanovitch; one does have such misfortunes."

"Only it's awfully funny all the same. But continue, continue, my dear friend!"

"Though I met you, too . . ."

"Stay! Why did you say 'manage that' just now? I meant to use a much more polite expression. But go on, go on!"

For some reason he felt more and more good-humoured. The feeling of shock was completely effaced by other emotions. He walked up and down the room with rapid steps.

"Even though I met you, and though when I set out for Petersburg I intended to seek you out, yet now, I repeat, I have been feeling so broken in spirit . . . and mentally shattered ever since March . . ."

"Oh, yes! shattered since March. . . . Stop a minute. Don't you smoke?"

"As you know, in old days when Natalya Vassilyevna was living I ..."

"To be sure, to be sure; and since March?"

"Just a cigarette, perhaps."

"Here is a cigarette. Light it—and go on! Go on, it's awfully——"

And, lighting a cigar, Velchaninov quickly settled himself on the bed again.

Pavel Pavlovitch paused.

"But how excited you are yourself. Are you quite in good health?"

"Oh, damn my health!" Velchaninov was suddenly exasperated. "Continue!"

The visitor, for his part, looking at his companion's agitation, seemed better pleased and grew more self-confident.

"But what is there to continue?" he began again. "Imagine, Alexey Ivanovitch, in the first place, a man destroyed—that is, not simply destroyed, but fundamentally, so to say; a man whose existence is transformed after twenty years of married life, wandering about the streets with no consistent object, as though in a wilderness, almost in a state of oblivion, and finding a certain fascination in that oblivion. It is natural that sometimes when I meet an acquaintance, even a real friend, I purposely go out of my way to avoid approaching him, at such a moment of oblivion, I mean. And at another moment one remembers everything so, and so longs to see any one who has witnessed that recent past, gone now never to return, and has taken part in it, and one's heart beats so violently that one is ready to risk throwing oneself upon a friend by night as well as by day, even though one might have to wake him up at four o'clock in the morning on purpose. . . . I have made a mistake about the time only, not about our friendship; for this moment more than makes up for it. And as for the time, I really thought it was only twelve, feeling as I do. One drinks the cup of one's sorrow till one is drunk with it. And it's not sorrow, indeed, but the novelty of my state that crushes me. . . ."

"How strangely you express yourself!" Velchaninov observed gloomily, becoming extremely grave again.

"Yes, I do express myself strangely. . . ."

"And you're . . . not joking?"

"Joking!" exclaimed Pavel Pavlovitch in pained surprise, "and at the moment when I am announcing the sad . . ."

"Ach, don't speak of that, I entreat you!"

Velchaninov got up and began pacing the room again.

So passed five minutes. The visitor seemed about to get up too, but Velchaninov shouted: "Sit still, sit still!" and Pavel Pavlovitch obediently sank back into his arm-chair at once.

"But, how you have changed though," Velchaninov began again, suddenly stopping before him as though all at once struck by the thought. "You're dreadfully changed! Extraordinarily! Quite a different person."

"That's not strange: nine years."

"No, no, no, it's not a question of years! It's incredible how you've changed in appearance; you've become a different man!"

"That, too, may well be, in nine years."

"Or is it since March!"

"He—he!" Pavel Pavlovitch sniggered slyly. "That's a funny idea of yours. . . . But if I may venture—what is the change exactly?"

"You ask what! The Pavel Pavlovitch I used to know was such a solid, decorous person, that Pavel Pavlovitch was such a clever chap, and now—this Pavel Pavlovitch is a regular *vaurien!*"

He was at that stage of irritability in which even reserved people say more than they ought.

"*Vaurien!*★ You think so? And not a clever chap now—not clever?" Pavel Pavlovitch chuckled with relish.

"Clever chap be damned! Now I daresay you really are too clever."

"I'm insolent, but this low fellow's more so and . . . and what is his object?" Velchaninov was thinking all the while.

"Ach, dearest, most precious friend!" cried the visitor suddenly, growing extremely agitated and turning round in his chair. "What are we saying? We are not in the world now, we're not in the society of the great and the worldly! We're two old friends, very old friends! And we've come together in the fullest sincerity to recall to one another the priceless bond of friendship of which the dear departed was the precious link!"

And he was so carried away by the ecstasy of his feeling that he bowed his head as before, hiding his face in his hat. Velchaninov watched him with aversion and uneasiness.

"What if he's simply a buffoon," flashed through his mind; "but n-no, n-no! I don't think he's drunk—he may be drunk, though: his face is red. Even if he were drunk—it comes to the same thing. What's he driving at? What does the low fellow want?"

"Do you remember, do you remember," cried Pavel Pavlovitch, removing the hat a little and seeming more and more carried away by his reminiscences, "do you remember our expeditions into the country, our evenings, and little parties with dancing and innocent games at the house of His Excellency, our most hospitable Semyon Semyonovitch? And how we used to read together, the three of us, in the evening! And our first acquaintance with you, when you called on me

---

★ Good-for-nothing.

that morning to make inquiries about your business, and even began to speak rather warmly, and suddenly Natalya Vassilyevna came in, and within ten minutes you had become a real friend of the family and so you were for a whole year, exactly as in Turgenev's play *A Provincial Lady*."

Velchaninov paced slowly up and down, looked at the floor, listened with impatience and repulsion, but—listened intently.

"The thought of *A Provincial Lady* never entered my head," he interrupted, somewhat confused, "and you never used to talk in such a shrill voice and such . . . unnatural language. What is that for?"

"I certainly used to be more silent—that is, I was more reserved," Pavel Pavlovitch interposed hurriedly. "You know I used to prefer listening while the dear departed talked. You remember how she used to talk, how wittily. . . . And in regard to *A Provincial Lady* and Stupendyev particularly, you are quite right, for I remember it was we ourselves, the precious departed and I, used to speak of that at quiet moments after you'd gone away—comparing our first meeting with that drama, for there really was a resemblance. About Stupendyev especially."

"What Stupendyev? Damn him!" cried Velchaninov, and he actually stamped, utterly disconcerted at the mention of "Stupendyev," owing to a disturbing recollection that was evoked by the name.

"Stupendyev is a character, a character in a play, the husband in *A Provincial Lady,*" Pavel Pavlovitch piped in a voice of honeyed sweetness; "but it belonged to a different series of our precious and happy memories, when after your departure Stepan Mihalovitch Bagautov bestowed his friendship on us, exactly as you did, for five whole years."

"Bagautov? What do you mean? What Bagautov?" Velchaninov stood still as though petrified.

"Bagautov, Stepan Mihalovitch, who bestowed his friendship on us, a year after you and . . . and exactly as you did."

"Good heavens, yes! I know that!" cried Velchaninov, recovering himself at last. "Bagautov! Why, of course, he had a berth in your town. . . ."

"He had, he had! At the Governor's! From Petersburg. A very elegant young man, belonging to the best society!" Pavel Pavlovitch exclaimed in a positive ecstasy.

"Yes, yes, yes! What was I thinking of? Why, he, too . . ."

"He too, he too," Pavel Pavlovitch repeated in the same ecstasy, catching up the word his companion had incautiously dropped. "He too! Well, we acted *A Provincial Lady* at His Excellency's, our most hospitable Semyon Semyonovitch's private theatre—Stepan

Mihalovitch was the 'count,' I was the 'husband,' and the dear departed was 'The Provincial Lady'—only they took away the 'husband's' part from me, Natalya Vassilyevna insisted on it, so that I did
not act the 'husband' because I was not fitted for the part. . . ."

"How the devil could you be Stupendyev? You're preeminently
Pavel Pavlovitch Trusotsky and not Stupendyev," said Velchaninov,
speaking with coarse rudeness and almost trembling with irritation.
"Only, excuse me; Bagautov's in Petersburg, I saw him myself in the
spring! Why don't you go and see him too?"

"I have been every blessed day, for the last fortnight. I'm not admitted! He's ill, he can't see me! And, only fancy, I've found out from
first-hand sources that he really is very dangerously ill! The friend of
six years. Ach, Alexey Ivanovitch, I tell you and I repeat it, that sometimes one's feelings are such that one longs to sink into the earth; yes,
really; at another moment one feels as though one could embrace any
one of those who have been, so to say, witnesses and participators of
the past and simply that one may weep, absolutely for nothing else but
that one may weep. . . ."

"Well, anyway, I've had enough of you for to-day, haven't I?"
Velchaninov brought out abruptly.

"More than enough, more!" Pavel Pavlovitch got up from his seat
at once. "It's four o'clock, and, what's worse, I have so selfishly upset
you. . . ."

"Listen, I will be sure to come and see you myself, and then, I hope
. . . Tell me straight out, tell me frankly, you are not drunk to-day?"

"Drunk! Not a bit of it. . . ."

"Hadn't you been drinking just before you came, or earlier?"

"Do you know, Alexey Ivanovitch, you're in a regular fever."

"I'll come and see you to-morrow morning before one o'clock."

"And I've been noticing for a long time that you seem, as it were,
delirious," Pavel Pavlovitch interrupted with zest, still harping on the
same subject. "I feel conscience-stricken, really, that by my awkwardness . . . but I'm going, I'm going! And you lie down and get some
sleep!"

"Why, you haven't told me where you're living," Velchaninov
called hastily after him.

"Didn't I tell you? At the Pokrovsky Hotel."

"What Pokrovsky Hotel?"

"Why, close to the Pokrovsky Church, close by, in the side street.
I've forgotten the name of the street and I've forgotten the number,
only it's close by the Pokrovsky Church."

"I shall find it!"

"You'll be very welcome."

He was by now on his way downstairs.

"Stay," Velchaninov shouted after him again; "you are not going to give me the slip?"

"How do you mean, give you the slip?" cried Pavel Pavlovitch, staring at him open-eyed and turning round to smile on the third step.

Instead of answering, Velchaninov shut the door with a loud slam, carefully locked it and fastened the hook. Returning to the room, he spat as though he had been in contact with something unclean.

After standing for some five minutes in the middle of the room, he flung himself on the bed without undressing and in one minute fell asleep. The forgotten candle burnt itself out on the table.

4. THE WIFE, THE HUSBAND
AND THE LOVER

He slept very soundly and woke up at half-past nine; he remembered everything instantly, sat down on his bed and began at once thinking of "that woman's death." The shock of the sudden news of that death the night before had left a certain agitation and even pain. That pain and agitation had only for a time been smothered by a strange idea while Pavel Pavlovitch was with him.

But now, on waking up, all that had happened nine years before rose before his mind with extraordinary vividness.

This woman, this Natalya Vassilyevna, the wife of "that Trusotsky," he had once loved, and he had been her lover for the whole year that he had spent at T——, ostensibly on business of his own (that, too, was a lawsuit over a disputed inheritance), although his presence had not really been necessary for so long. The real cause of his remaining was this intrigue. The *liaison* and his love had such complete possession of him that it was as though he were in bondage to Natalya Vassilyevna, and he would probably have been ready on the spot to do anything, however monstrous and senseless, to satisfy that woman's slightest caprice.

He had never felt anything of the sort before. At the end of the year, when separation was inevitable, although it was expected to be only a brief one, Velchaninov was in such despair, as the fatal time drew near, that he proposed to Natalya Vassilyevna that she should elope with him, that he should carry her off from her husband, that they should throw up everything and that she should come abroad with him for ever. Nothing but the jibes and firm determination of the lady (who had, probably from boredom, or to amuse herself, quite

approved of the project at first) could have dissuaded him and forced
him to go alone. And actually, before two months had passed, he was
asking himself in Petersburg the question which had always remained
unanswered. Had he really loved that woman or had it been nothing
but an "infatuation"? And it was not levity or the influence of some
new passion that had given rise to this question: for those first two
months in Petersburg he had been plunged in a sort of stupefaction
and had scarcely noticed any woman, although he had at once mixed
with his former acquaintances again and had seen a hundred women.
At the same time he knew that if he were transported that moment
to T—— he would promptly fall under the yoke of that woman's fascination again, in spite of any questions. Even five years later his conviction was unchanged. But five years later he used to admit this to
himself with indignation and he even thought of "that woman" herself with hatred. He was ashamed of that year at T——; he could not
even understand how such a "stupid" passion could have been possible for him, Velchaninov. All his memories of that passion had
become absurd to him; and he blushed to the point of tears and was
tormented by conscience-pricks at the thought of it. It is true that a
few years later he had become somewhat calmer; he tried to forget it
all—and almost succeeded. And now, all at once, nine years afterwards,
all this had so suddenly and strangely risen up before him again, after
hearing that night of the death of Natalya Vassilyevna.

Now, sitting on his bed, with confused thoughts crowding in disorder on his mind, he felt and realized clearly one thing only—that in
spite of the "shock" he had felt at the news, he was nevertheless quite
undisturbed by the fact of her death. "Can it be that I have no feeling for her?" he asked himself. It is true that he had now no feeling
of hatred for her, and that he could criticize her more impartially,
more fairly. In the course of those nine years of separation he had long
since formulated the view that Natalya Vassilyevna belonged to the
class of absolutely ordinary provincial ladies moving in good provincial society "and, who knows? perhaps she really was such, perhaps it
was only I who idealized her so fantastically." He had always suspected, however, that there might be an error in that view; and he felt
it even now. And, indeed, the facts were opposed to it; this Bagautov,
too, had for several years been connected with her and apparently he,
too, had been "under the yoke of her fascination." Bagautov certainly
was a young man belonging to the best Petersburg society and, as he
was a most "empty-headed fellow," he could only have had a successful career in Petersburg (Velchaninov used to say of him). Yet he had
neglected Petersburg—that is, sacrificed his most important interests—and remained for five years in T—— solely on account of that

woman! Yes, and he had finally returned to Petersburg, perhaps only because he, too, had been cast off like "an old, worn-out shoe." So there must have been in that woman something exceptional—a power of attracting, of enslaving, of dominating.

And yet one would have thought that she had not the gifts with which to attract and to enslave. She was not exactly pretty; perhaps she was actually plain. She was twenty-eight when Velchaninov first knew her. Though not altogether beautiful, her face was sometimes charmingly animated, but her eyes were not pretty: there was something like an excess of determination in them. She was very thin. On the intellectual side she had not been well educated; her keen intelligence was unmistakable, though she was one-sided in her ideas. Her manners were those of a provincial lady and at the same time, it is true, she had a great deal of tact; she had artistic taste, but showed it principally in knowing how to dress. In character she was resolute and domineering; she could never make up her mind to compromise in anything: it was all or nothing. In difficult positions her firmness and stoicism were amazing. She was capable of generosity and at the same time would be utterly unjust. To argue with that lady was impossible: "twice two makes four" meant nothing to her. She never thought herself wrong or to blame in anything. Her continual deception of her husband and the perfidies beyond number which she practised upon him did not weigh on her in the least. But, to quote Velchaninov's own comparison, she was like the "Madonna of the Flagellants," who believes implicitly herself that she is the mother of God—so Natalya Vassilyevna believed implicitly in everything she did.

She was faithful to her lover, but only as long as he did not bore her. She was fond of tormenting her lover, but she liked making up for it too. She was of a passionate, cruel and sensual type. She hated depravity and condemned it with exaggerated severity and—was herself depraved. No sort of fact could have made her recognize her own depravity. "Most likely she *genuinely* does not know it," Velchaninov thought about her even before he left T——. (We may remark, by the way, that he was the accomplice of her depravity.) "She is one of those women who are born to be unfaithful wives. Such women never become old maids; it's a law of their nature to be married to that end. The husband is the first lover, but never till after the wedding. No one gets married more adroitly and easily than this type of woman. For her first infidelity the husband is always to blame. And it is all accompanied by the most perfect sincerity: to the end they feel themselves absolutely right and, of course, entirely innocent."

Velchaninov was convinced that there really was such a type of woman; but, on the other hand, he was also convinced that there was a type of husband corresponding to that woman, whose sole vocation was to correspond with that feminine type. To his mind, the essence of such a husband lay in his being, so to say, "the eternal husband," or rather in being, all his life, a husband and nothing more. "Such a man is born and grows up only to be a husband, and, having married, is promptly transformed into a supplement of his wife, even when he happens to have unmistakable character of his own. The chief sign of such a husband is a certain decoration. He can no more escape wearing horns than the sun can help shining; he is not only unaware of the fact, but is bound by the very laws of his nature to be unaware of it." Velchaninov firmly believed in the existence of these two types and in Pavel Pavlovitch Trusotsky's being a perfect representative of one of them. The Pavel Pavlovitch of the previous night was, of course, very different from the Pavel Pavlovitch he had known at T——. He found him incredibly changed, but Velchaninov knew that he was bound to have changed and that all that was perfectly natural; Trusotsky could only as long as his wife was alive have remained all that he used to be, but, as it was, he was only a fraction of a whole, suddenly cut off and set free; that is, something wonderful and unique.

As for the Pavel Pavlovitch of the past at T——, this is how Velchaninov remembered him and recalled him now.

"Of course, at T——, Pavel Pavlovitch had been simply a husband," and nothing more. If he were, for instance, an official in the service as well, it was solely because such a position was one of the obligations of his married life; he was in the service for the sake of his wife and her social position in T——, though he was in himself zealous in his duties. He was thirty-five then and was possessed of some little fortune. He showed no special ability in his department and showed no special lack of it either. He used to mix with all the best people in the province and was said to be on an excellent footing with them. Natalya Vassilyevna was deeply respected in T——; she did not, however, greatly appreciate that, accepting it as simply her due, but in her own house she was superb at entertaining guests, and Pavel Pavlovitch had been so well trained by her that he was able to behave with dignity even when entertaining the highest magnates of the province. Perhaps (it seemed to Velchaninov) he had intelligence too, but as Natalya Vassilyevna did not like her spouse to talk too much, his intelligence was not very noticeable. Perhaps he had many natural good qualities, as well as bad ones. But his good qualities were kept under a shade, as it were, and his evil propensities were almost completely stifled.

Velchaninov remembered, for instance, that Pavel Pavlovitch sometimes betrayed a disposition to laugh at his neighbours, but this was sternly forbidden him. He was fond, too, at times of telling anecdotes;

but a watch was kept on that weakness too, and he was only allowed to tell such as were brief and of little importance. He had a weakness for a festive glass outside the house and was even capable of drinking too much with a friend; but this failing had been severely nipped in the bud. And it is noteworthy that no outside observer would have said that Pavel Pavlovitch was a hen-pecked husband; Natalya Vassilyevna seemed an absolutely obedient wife, and most likely believed herself to be one. It was possible that Pavel Pavlovitch loved Natalya Vassilyevna passionately; but no one noticed it, and, indeed, it was impossible to notice it, and this reserve was probably due to her domestic discipline. Several times during his life at T—— Velchaninov had asked himself whether the husband had any suspicion at all of his wife's intrigue. Several times he questioned Natalya Vassilyevna seriously about it, and always received the answer, uttered with a certain annoyance, that her husband knew nothing and never could know anything about it and that "it was no concern of his." Another characteristic of hers was that she never laughed at Pavel Pavlovitch and did not consider him absurd or very plain and would, indeed, have taken his part very warmly if any one had dared to show him incivility. Having no children, she was naturally bound to become a society woman, but her home life, too, was essential to her. Social pleasures never had complete sway of her, and at home she was very fond of needlework and looking after the house. Pavel Pavlovitch had recalled, that night, the evenings they had spent in reading; it happened that sometimes Velchaninov read aloud and sometimes Pavel Pavlovitch: to Velchaninov's surprise he read aloud excellently. Meanwhile, Natalya Vassilyevna did sewing as she listened, always calmly and serenely. They read a novel of Dickens, something from a Russian magazine, sometimes even something "serious." Natalya Vassilyevna highly appreciated Velchaninov's culture, but appreciated it in silence, as something final and established, of which there was no need to talk. Altogether, her attitude to everything intellectual and literary was rather one of indifference, as to something irrelevant though perhaps useful. Pavel Pavlovitch sometimes showed considerable warmth on the subject.

The *liaison* at T—— was broken suddenly when on Velchaninov's side it had reached its zenith—that is, almost the point of madness. In reality he was abruptly dismissed, though it was all so arranged that he went away without grasping that he had been cast off "like a worthless old shoe."

Six weeks before his departure, a young artillery officer who had just finished at the training college arrived in T—— and took to visiting the Trusotskys. Instead of three, they were now a party of four.

Natalya Vassilyevna welcomed the boy graciously but treated him as a boy. No suspicion crossed Velchaninov's mind and indeed he had no thought to spare for it, for he had just been told that separation was inevitable. One of the hundreds of reasons urged by Natalya Vassilyevna for his leaving her as soon as possible was that she believed herself to be with child: and therefore, naturally, he must disappear at once for three or four months at least, so that it would not be so easy for her husband to feel any doubt if there were any kind of gossip afterwards. It was rather a far-fetched argument. After a stormy proposition on the part of Velchaninov that she should fly with him to Paris or America, he departed alone to Petersburg, "only for a brief moment, of course," that is, for no more than three months, or nothing would have induced him to go, in spite of any reason or argument. Exactly two months later he received in Petersburg a letter from Natalya Vassilyevna asking him never to return, as she already loved another; she informed him that she had been mistaken about her condition. This information was superfluous. It was all clear to him now: he remembered the young officer. With that it was all over for good. He chanced to hear afterwards, some years later, that Bagautov had appeared on the scene and spent five whole years there. He explained the disproportionate duration of that affair partly by the fact that Natalya Vassilyevna, by now, was a good deal older, and so more constant in her attachments.

He remained sitting on his bed for nearly an hour: at last he roused himself, rang for Mavra to bring his coffee, drank it hastily, and at eleven o'clock set out to look for the Pokrovsky Hotel. In going there he had a special idea which had only come to him in the morning. He felt somewhat ashamed of his behaviour to Pavel Pavlovitch the night before and now he wanted to efface the impression.

The whole fantastic business with the door handle, the night before, he now put down to chance, to the tipsy condition of Pavel Pavlovitch and perhaps to something else, but he did not really know, exactly, why he was going now to form new relations with the former husband, when everything had so naturally and of its own accord ended between them. Something attracted him. He had received a peculiar impression and he was attracted in consequence of it.

5. LIZA

Pavel Pavlovitch had no idea of "giving him the slip," and goodness knows why Velchaninov had asked him the question the night before;

he was, indeed, at a loss to explain it himself. At his first inquiry at a little shop near the Pokrovsky Church, he was directed to the hotel in the side street a couple of paces away. At the hotel, it was explained that M. Trusotsky was staying in the lodge close by in the courtyard, in furnished rooms at Marya Sysoevna's. Going up the narrow, wet and very dirty stone stairs to the second storey, where these rooms were, he suddenly heard the sound of crying. It seemed like the crying of a child of seven or eight; the sound was distressing; he heard smothered sobs which would break out and with them the stamping of feet and shouts of fury, which were smothered, too, in a hoarse falsetto voice, evidently that of a grown-up man. This man seemed to be trying to suppress the child and to be very anxious that her crying should not be heard, but was making more noise than she was. The shouts sounded pitiless, and the child seemed to be begging forgiveness. In a small passage at the top, with doors on both sides of it, Velchaninov met a tall, stout, slovenly-looking peasant woman of forty and asked for Pavel Pavlovitch. She pointed towards the door from which the sounds were coming. There was a look of some indignation on the fat, purple face of this woman.

"You see how he amuses himself!" she said gruffly and went downstairs.

Velchaninov was just about to knock at the door, but on second thoughts he walked straight in. In a small room, roughly though amply furnished with common painted furniture, stood Pavel Pavlovitch without his coat and waistcoat. With a flushed and exasperated face he was trying, by means of shouts, gesticulations and even (Velchaninov fancied) kicks, to silence a little girl of eight, shabbily dressed in a short, black, woollen frock. She seemed to be actually in hysterics, she gasped hysterically and held out her hands to Pavel Pavlovitch as though she wanted to clutch at him, to hug him, to beseech and implore him about something. In one instant the whole scene was transformed: seeing the visitor, the child cried out and dashed away into a tiny room adjoining, and Pavel Pavlovitch, for a moment disconcerted, instantly melted into smiles, exactly as he had done the night before when Velchaninov flung open the door upon him on the stairs.

"Alexey Ivanovitch!" he cried, in genuine surprise. "I could never have expected ... but come in, come in! Here, on the sofa, or here in the arm-chair, while I ..."

And he rushed to put on his coat, forgetting to put on his waistcoat.

"Stay as you are, don't stand on ceremony."

Velchaninov sat down in the chair.

"No, allow me to stand on ceremony; here, now I am more respectable. But why are you sitting in the corner? Sit here in the armchair, by the table. . . . Well, I didn't expect you, I didn't expect you!"

He, too, sat down on the edge of a rush-bottomed chair, not beside his "unexpected" visitor, but setting his chair at an angle so as to sit more nearly facing him.

"Why didn't you expect me? Why, I told you last night that I would come at this time."

"I thought you wouldn't come; and when I reflected on all that happened yesterday, on waking this morning, I despaired of ever seeing you again."

Meanwhile Velchaninov was looking about him. The room was in disorder, the bed was not made, clothes were lying about, on the table were glasses with dregs of coffee in them, crumbs and a bottle of champagne, half full, with the cork out and a glass beside it. He stole a glance towards the next room, but there all was quiet; the child was in hiding and perfectly still.

"Surely you are not drinking that now?" said Velchaninov, indicating the champagne.

"The remains . . ." said Pavel Pavlovitch in confusion.

"Well, you have changed!"

"It's a bad habit, come upon me all at once; yes, really, since that date. I'm not lying! I can't restrain myself. Don't be uneasy, Alexey Ivanovitch. I'm not drunk now, and I'm not going to play the fool now as I did at your flat yesterday; but I'm telling the truth, it's all since then. And if any one had told me six months ago that I should break down like this, if I'd been shown myself in the looking-glass—I shouldn't have believed it."

"You were drunk last night, then?"

"I was," Pavel Pavlovitch admitted in a low voice, looking down in embarrassment. "And you see I wasn't exactly drunk then, but I had been a little before. I want to explain, because I'm always worse a little while after. If I get ever so little tipsy, it is followed by a sort of violence and foolishness, and I feel my grief more intensely too. It's because of my grief, perhaps, I drink. Then I'm capable of playing all sorts of pranks and I push myself forward quite stupidly and insult people for nothing. I must have presented myself very strangely to you yesterday?"

"Do you mean to say you don't remember?"

"Not remember! I remember it all. . . ."

"You see, Pavel Pavlovitch, that's just what I thought," Velchaninov said in a conciliatory voice. "What's more, I was myself rather irritable with you last night and . . . too impatient, I readily admit it. I don't feel quite well at times, and then your unexpected arrival last night . . ."

"Yes, at night, at night!" Pavel Pavlovitch shook his head, as though surprised and disapproving. "And what possessed me! Nothing would have induced me to come in to you if you had not opened the door yourself; I should have gone away from the door. I came to you a week ago, Alexey Ivanovitch, and you were not at home, but perhaps I should never have come again. I have some pride, too, Alexey Ivanovitch, although I do recognize the position I am in. We met in the street, too, and I kept thinking: 'Why, he must recognize me and yet he turns away; nine years are no joke,' and I couldn't make up my mind to come. And last night I had wandered from the Petersburg Side and I forgot the time. It all came from that" (he pointed to the bottle), "and from my feelings. It was stupid! Very! And if it had been any one but you—for you've come to see me even after what happened yesterday, for the sake of old times—I should have given up all hope of renewing our acquaintance!"

Velchaninov listened attentively. The man seemed to him to be speaking sincerely and even with a certain dignity; and yet he did not believe one word he had heard since he came into the room.

"Tell me, Pavel Pavlovitch, you are not alone here, then? Whose little girl is that I found with you just now?"

Pavel Pavlovitch was positively amazed and raised his eyebrows, but he looked frankly and pleasantly at Velchaninov.

"Whose little girl? Why, it's Liza!" he said, with an affable smile.

"What Liza?" muttered Velchaninov, with a sort of inward tremor. The shock was too sudden. When he came in and saw Liza, just before, he was surprised, but had absolutely no presentiment of the truth, and thought nothing particular about her.

"Yes, our Liza, our daughter Liza!" Pavel Pavlovitch smiled.

"Your daughter? Do you mean that you and Natalya . . . Natalya Vassilyevna had children?" Velchaninov asked timidly and mistrustfully, in a very low voice.

"Why, of course! But there, upon my word, how should you have heard of it? What am I thinking about! It was after you went away, God blessed us with her!"

Pavel Pavlovitch positively jumped up from his chair in some agitation, though it seemed agreeable too.

"I heard nothing about it," said Velchaninov, and he turned pale.

"To be sure, to be sure; from whom could you have heard it?" said Pavel Pavlovitch, in a voice weak with emotion. "My poor wife and I had lost all hope, as no doubt you remember, and suddenly God sent us this blessing, and what it meant to me—He only knows! Just a year after you went away, I believe. No, not a year, not nearly a year. Wait a bit; why, you left us, if my memory does not deceive me, in October or November, I believe."

"I left T—— at the beginning of September, the twelfth of September; I remember it very well."

"In September, was it? H'm! . . . what was I thinking about?" cried Pavel Pavlovitch, much surprised. "Well, if that's so, let me see: you went away on the twelfth of September, and Liza was born on the eighth of May, so—September—October—November—December—January—February—March—April—a little over eight months! And if you only knew how my poor wife . . ."

"Show me . . . call her . . ." Velchaninov faltered in a breaking voice.

"Certainly!" said Pavel Pavlovitch fussily, at once breaking off what he was saying, as though it were of no consequence. "Directly, directly, I'll introduce her!"

And he went hurriedly into the other room to Liza.

Fully three or perhaps four minutes passed; there was a hurried, rapid whispering in the room, and he just caught the sound of Liza's voice. "She's begging not to be brought in," thought Velchaninov. At last they came out.

"You see, she's all confusion," said Pavel Pavlovitch; "she's so shy, and so proud . . . the image of my poor wife!"

Liza came in, looking down and no longer tearful; her father was holding her hand. She was a tall, slim, very pretty little girl. She raised her big blue eyes to glance with curiosity at the visitor, looked at him sullenly, and dropped them again at once. Her eyes were full of that gravity one sees in children when they are left alone with a stranger and, retreating into a corner, look out solemnly and mistrustfully at the unfamiliar visitor; but she had, perhaps, some other thought, by no means childish, in her mind—so Velchaninov fancied.

Her father led her straight up to him.

"This is an uncle Mother used to know long ago; he was our friend. Don't be shy, hold out your hand."

The child bent forward a little, and timidly held out her hand.

"Natalya Vassilyevna would not have her trained to curtsey, but taught her to make a little bow, and hold out her hand in the English fashion," he added by way of explanation to Velchaninov, watching him intently.

Velchaninov knew that he was being watched, but had quite ceased to trouble himself to conceal his emotion; he sat perfectly still in this chair, held Liza's hand in his and gazed at the child. But Liza was in great anxiety about something, and, forgetting her hand in the visitor's hand, she kept her eyes fixed on her father. She listened apprehensively to all that he said. Velchaninov recognized those big blue eyes at once, but what struck him most of all was the wonderful soft whiteness of her face and the colour of her hair; these characteristics were so marked and so significant. Her features and the lines of the lips reminded him vividly of Natalya Vassilyevna. Meanwhile, Pavel Pavlovitch had for some time been telling him something, speaking, it seemed, with very great warmth and feeling, but Velchaninov did not hear him. He only caught the last sentence—

". . . so that you can't imagine our joy at this gift from the Lord, Alexey Ivanovitch! She became everything to me as soon as she came to us, so that I used to think that even if my tranquil happiness should, by God's will, be at an end, Liza would always be left me; that I reckoned upon for certain!"

"And Natalya Vassilyevna?" Velchaninov queried.

"Natalya Vassilyevna?" said Pavel Pavlovitch affectedly. "You know her way, you remember that she never cared to say a great deal, but the way she said good-bye to her on her death-bed . . . everything came out then! I said just now 'on her death-bed,' but yet only a day before her death she was upset and angry, said that they were trying to cure her with drugs, that there was nothing wrong with her but an ordinary fever, and that neither of our doctors understood it, and that as soon as Koch came back (do you remember our old friend the army doctor?) she would be up again in a fortnight! But there! five hours before her decease she remembered that in three weeks' time we must visit her aunt, Liza's godmother, on her name day . . ."

Velchaninov suddenly got up from his chair, still holding the child's hand. Among other things it struck him that there was something reproachful in the intense look the child kept fixed upon her father.

"She's not ill?" he asked hurriedly and somewhat strangely.

"I don't think so, but . . . our circumstances are here so . . ." said Pavel Pavlovitch, with mournful solicitude. "She's a strange child and nervous at all times; after her mother's death she was ill for a fortnight, hysterical. Why, what a weeping and wailing we had just before you came in . . . do you hear, Liza, do you hear? And what was it all about? All because I go out and leave her; she says it shows I don't love her any more as I used to when mother was alive—that's her complaint against me. And a child like that who ought to be playing with her toys, instead of fretting over a fantastic notion like that. Though here she has no one to play with."

"Why, how . . . you're surely not alone here?"

"Quite alone; the servant only comes in once a day."

"And you go out and leave her like this alone?"

"What else could I do? And when I went out yesterday I locked her in, into that little room there, that's what the tears have been about to-day. But what else could I do? Judge for yourself: the day before yesterday she went down when I was out, and a boy threw a stone at her in the yard and hit her on the head. Or else she begins crying and runs round to all the lodgers in the yard, asking where I've gone. And that's not nice, you know. And I'm a nice one, too; I go out for an hour and come back next morning; that's what happened yesterday. It was a nice thing, too, that while I was away the landlady let her out, sent for a locksmith to break the lock—such a disgrace—I literally feel myself a monster. All mental aberration, all mental aberration. . . ."

"Father!" the child said timidly and uneasily.

"There you are, at it again! You're at the same thing again. What did I tell you just now?"

"I won't, I won't!" Liza repeated in terror, hurriedly clasping her hands before him.

"You can't go on like this in these surroundings," Velchaninov said impatiently, in a voice of authority. "Why, you . . . why, you're a man of property; how is it you're living like this—in this lodge and in such surroundings?"

"In the lodge? But, you see, we may be going away in a week's time, and we've wasted a great deal of money already, even though I have property. . . ."

"Come, that's enough, that's enough." Velchaninov cut him short with increasing impatience, as it were expressing plainly "There's no need to talk. I know all that you have to say, and I know with what feelings you are speaking."

"Listen, I'll make a suggestion. You said just now that you'll be staying a week, maybe possibly even a fortnight. I know a household here, that is, a family where I'm quite at home—have known them twenty years. The father, Alexandr Pavlovitch Pogoryeltsev, is a Privy Councillor; he might be of use to you in your business. They are at their summer villa now. They've got a splendid villa. Klavdia Petrovna is like a sister to me or a mother. They have eight children. Let me take Liza to them at once . . . that we may lose no time. They will be delighted to take her in for the whole time you are here, and will treat her like their own child, their own child!"

He was terribly impatient and did not disguise it.

"That's scarcely possible," said Pavel Pavlovitch, with a grimace, looking, so Velchaninov fancied, slily in his face.

"Why, why impossible?"

"Why, how can I let the child go so suddenly—with such a real friend as you, of course—I don't mean, but into a house of strangers, and of such high rank, where I don't know how she'd be received either?"

"But I've told you that I'm like one of the family!" cried Velchaninov, almost wrathfully. "Klavdia Petrovna will be delighted to take her at a word from me—as though it were my child. Damn it all! Why, you know yourself that you only say all this for the sake of saying something . . . there's nothing to discuss!"

He positively stamped his foot.

"I only mean, won't it seem strange? I should have to go and see her once or twice anyway, or she would be left without a father! He—he! . . . and in such a grand household."

"But it's the simplest household, not 'grand' at all!" shouted Velchaninov. "I tell you there are a lot of children. She's revive there, that's the whole object. . . . And I'll introduce you myself to-morrow, if you like. And of course you would have to go to thank them; we'll drive over every day, if you like."

"It's all so . . ."

"Nonsense! And, what's more, you know that yourself! Listen. Come to me this evening, and stay the night, perhaps, and we'll set off early in the morning so as to get there at twelve."

"My benefactor! And even to stay the night with you . . ." Pavel Pavlovitch agreed suddenly in a tone of fervent feeling. "You are doing me a charity literally. . . . Where is their villa?"

"Their villa is in Lyesnoe."

"Only, I say, what about her dress? For, you know, in such a distinguished household and in their summer villa, too, you know yourself . . . a father's heart . . ."

"What about her dress? She's in mourning. She couldn't be dressed differently, could she? It's the most suitable one could possibly imagine! The only thing is she ought to have clean linen . . . a clean tucker . . ."

Her tucker and what showed of her underlinen were, in fact, very dirty.

"She must change her things at once," said Pavel Pavlovitch fussily, "and we'll get together the rest of what she needs in the way of underclothes; Marya Sysoevna has got them in the wash."

"Then you should tell them to fetch a carriage," Velchaninov interposed; "and make haste if you can."

But a difficulty presented itself: Liza resolutely opposed it; she had been listening all the time in terror, and, if Velchaninov had had time to look at her attentively while he was persuading Pavel Pavlovitch, he would have seen a look of utter despair upon her little face.

"I am not going," she said firmly, in a low voice.

"There, there! You see, she's her mother over again."

"I'm not my mother over again, I'm not my mother over again!" cried Liza in despair, wringing her little hands, and as it were trying to defend herself before her father from the awful reproach of being like her mother. "Father, Father, if you leave me . . ."

She suddenly turned on Velchaninov, who was in dismay.

"If you take me I'll . . ."

But before she had time to say more, Pavel Pavlovitch clutched her by the arm and with undisguised exasperation dragged her almost by the collar into the little room. Whispering followed for some minutes; there was the sound of suppressed crying. Velchaninov was on the point of going in himself, but Pavel Pavlovitch came out and with a wry smile announced that she was coming directly. Velchaninov tried not to look at him and kept his eyes turned away.

Marya Sysoevna appeared. She was the same peasant woman that he had met just before in the passage; she began packing the linen she had brought with her in a pretty little bag belonging to Liza.

"Are you taking the little girl away then, sir?" she asked, addressing Velchaninov. "Have you a family, then? It's a good deed, sir: she's a quiet child; you are taking her from a perfect Bedlam."

"Come, come, Marya Sysoevna!" muttered Pavel Pavlovitch.

"Marya Sysoevna, indeed! That's my name, right enough. It is a Bedlam here, isn't it? Is it the proper thing for a child that can understand to see such disgraceful goings-on? They've fetched you a carriage, sir—to Lyesnoe, is it?"

"Yes, yes."

"Well, it's a blessing you came!"

Liza came out pale and, looking down, took her bag. Not one glance in Velchaninov's direction; she restrained herself and did not, as before, rush to embrace her father, even at parting; evidently she was unwilling to look at him either. Her father kissed her decorously on the head and patted it; her lips twitched as he did so and her little chin quivered, but still she did not raise her eyes to her father. Pavel Pavlovitch looked pale, and his hands were trembling—Velchaninov noticed that distinctly, though he was doing his utmost not to look at him. The one thing he longed for was to get away as quickly as possible.

"After all, it's not my fault," he thought. "It was bound to be so."

They went downstairs; there Marya Sysoevna kissed Liza good-bye, and only when she was sitting in the carriage Liza lifted her eyes to her father, flung up her hands and screamed; another minute and she would have flung herself out of the carriage to him, but the horses had started.

6. A NEW FANCY OF AN IDLE MAN

"Are you feeling ill?" asked Velchaninov in alarm. "I will tell them to stop, I'll tell them to bring water. . . ."

She turned her eyes upon him and looked at him passionately, reproachfully.

"Where are you taking me?" she asked sharply and abruptly.

"It's a very nice family, Liza. They're in a delightful summer villa now; there are a lot of children; they'll love you; they are kind. Don't be angry with me, Liza; I only wish for your good."

How strange it would have seemed to all who knew him if any one could have seen him at that moment.

"How . . . how . . . how . . . how horrid you are!" said Liza, choking with stifled tears, glaring at him with her beautiful eyes full of anger.

"Liza, I . . ."

"You are wicked, wicked, wicked, wicked!"

She wrung her hands. Velchaninov was completely at a loss.

"Liza, darling, if you knew how despairing you make me!"

"Is it true that he will come to-morrow? Is it true?" she asked peremptorily.

"Yes, yes, I'll bring him myself; I'll take him with me and bring him."

"He'll deceive me," she whispered, looking down.

"Doesn't he love you, Liza?"

"He doesn't love me."

"Does he ill-treat you? Does he?"

Liza looked at him gloomily and was mute. She turned away from him again and sat with her eyes obstinately cast down. He began trying to coax her; he talked to her warmly, he was in a perfect fever. Liza listened with mistrust and hostility, but she did listen. Her attention delighted him extremely; he even began explaining to her what was meant by a man's drinking. He told her that he loved her himself and would look after her father. Liza lifted her eyes at last and looked at him intently. He began telling her how he used to know her mother and he saw that what he told her interested her. Little by little she began answering his questions, though cautiously and in monosyllables. She still stubbornly refused to answer his leading questions; she remained obstinately silent about everything to do with her relations with her father in the past. As he talked to her, Velchaninov took her hand in his as before and held it; she did not pull it away. The child was not silent all the time, however; she let out in her confused answers that she loved her father more than her mother, because he had always been fonder of her, and her mother had not cared so much for her, but that when her mother was dying she had kissed her and cried a great deal when every one had gone out of the room and they were left alone . . . and that now she loved her more than any one, more than any one, more than any one in the world, and every night she loved her more than any one. But the child was certainly proud. Realizing that she had spoken too freely, she suddenly shrank into herself again and glanced with positive hatred at Velchaninov, who had led her into saying so much. Towards the end of the journey her hysterical agitation almost passed off, but she sank into brooding and had the look of a wild creature, sullen and gloomily, resolutely stubborn. The fact that she was being taken to a strange family, in which she had never been before, seemed for the time being not to trouble her much. What tormented her was something else.

Velchaninov saw that; he guessed that she was ashamed before *him*, that she was ashamed of her father's having so easily let her go with him, of his having, as it were, flung her into his keeping.

"She is ill," he thought, "perhaps very ill; she's been worried to death. . . . Oh, the drunken, abject beast! I understand him now!"

He urged on the driver; he rested his hopes on the country, the fresh air, the garden, the children, and the new, unfamiliar life, and then, later on . . . But of what would come afterwards he had no doubts at all; of the future he had the fullest, brightest hopes. One thing only he knew for certain: that he had never before felt what he was experiencing now and that it would never leave him all his life.

"Here was an object, here was life!" he thought triumphantly.

A great many thoughts flashed upon his mind, but he did not dwell upon them and obstinately put away details; so long as he avoided details it all seemed clear and unassailable. His plan of action was self-evident.

"It will be possible to work upon that wretch," he mused, "by our united forces, and he will leave Liza in Petersburg at the Pogoryeltsevs', though at first only temporarily, for a certain time, and will go away alone, and Liza will be left to me; that's the whole thing. What more do I want? And . . . of course, he wants that himself; or else why does he torment her?"

At last they arrived. The Pogoryeltsevs' country home really was a charming place; they were met first of all by a noisy crowd of children, flocking out into the porch. Velchaninov had not been there for a long time, and the children were in a frenzy of delight; they were fond of him. The elder ones shouted to him at once, before he got out of the carriage—

"And how about the case, how is your case getting on?"

The cry was caught up even by the smallest, and they shrieked it mirthfully in imitation of their elders. They used to tease him about the lawsuit. But, seeing Liza, they surrounded her at once and began scrutinizing her with intent, dumb, childish curiosity. Klavdia Petrovna came out, followed by her husband. She and her husband, too, began with a laughing question about the lawsuit.

Klavdia Petrovna was a lady about thirty-seven, a plump and still good-looking brunette, with a fresh, rosy face. Her husband was fifty-five, a shrewd and clever man, but above everything good-natured. Their house was in the fullest sense of the word "a home" to Velchaninov, as he had said himself. But underlying this was the special circumstance that, twenty years before, Klavdia Petrovna had been on the point of marrying Velchaninov, then a student, hardly more than a boy. It was a case of first love, ardent, ridiculous and splendid. It had ended, however, in her marrying Pogoryeltsev. Five years later they had met again, and it had all ended in a quiet, serene friendship. A certain warmth, a peculiar glow suffusing their relations, had remained for ever. All was pure and irreproachable in Velchaninov's memories of this friendship, and it was the dearer to him for being perhaps the solitary case in which this was so. Here in this family he was simple, unaffected and kind; he used to fondle the children, he admitted all his failings, confessed his shortcomings, and never gave himself airs. He swore more than once to the Pogoryeltsevs that he should before long give up the world, come and live with them and never leave them again. In his heart he thought of this project seriously.

He told them all that was necessary about Liza in some detail; but a mere request from him was enough, without any special explanations. Klavdia Petrovna kissed the "orphan" and promised for her part to do everything. The children took possession of Liza and carried her off to play in the garden.

After half an hour of lively conversation Velchaninov got up and began saying good-bye. He was so impatient that every one noticed it. They were all astonished; he had not been to see them for three weeks and now he was going in half an hour. He laughed and pledged himself to come next day. They remarked that he seemed to be in a state of great excitement; he suddenly took Klavdia Petrovna's hand and, on the pretext of having forgotten to tell her something important, drew her aside into another room.

"Do you remember what I told you—you alone—what even your husband does not know—of my year at T——?"

"I remember perfectly; you often talked of it."

"It was not talking, it was a confession, to you alone, to you alone!

I never told you the surname of that woman; she was the wife of this man Trusotsky. She is dead, and Liza is her daughter—my daughter!"

"Is it certain? You are not mistaken?" Klavdia Petrovna asked with some excitement.

"It's perfectly certain, perfectly certain; I am not mistaken!" Velchaninov pronounced ecstatically.

And as briefly as he could, in haste and great excitement, he told her everything. Klavdia Petrovna already knew the whole story, but not the lady's name.

Velchaninov had always been so alarmed at the very idea that any one who knew him might ever meet Madame Trusotsky and think that *he* could *so* have loved that woman, that he had not till that day dared to reveal "that woman's" name even to Klavdia Petrovna, his one friend.

"And the father knows nothing?" asked Klavdia Petrovna, when she had heard his story.

"Y-yes, he does know. . . . It worries me that I've not got to the bottom of it yet!" Velchaninov went on eagerly. "He knows, he knows; I noticed it to-day and yesterday. But I must know how much he knows. That's why I'm in a hurry now. He is coming to me this evening. I can't imagine, though, how he can have found out—found out *everything,* I mean. He knows about Bagautov, there's no doubt of that. But about me? You know how clever women are in reassuring their husbands in such cases! If an angel came down from heaven—the husband would not believe him, but he would believe his wife! Don't shake your head and don't blame me; I blame myself and have blamed myself, for the whole affair, long ago, long ago! . . . You see, I was so certain he knew when I was there this morning that I compromised myself before him. Would you believe it, I felt so wretched and ashamed at having met him so rudely yesterday (I will tell you all about it fully afterwards). He came to me yesterday from an irresistible, malicious desire to let me know that he knew of the wrong done him, and knew who had done it; that was the whole reason of his stupid visit when he was drunk. But that was so natural on his part! He simply came to work off his resentment! I was altogether too hasty with him this morning and yesterday! Careless—stupid! I betrayed myself to him. Why did he turn up at a moment when I was upset? I tell you he's even been tormenting Liza, tormenting the child, and probably that, too, was to work off his resentment—to vent his malice if only on the child! Yes, he is spiteful—insignificant as he is, yet he is spiteful; very much so, indeed. In himself he is no more than a buffoon, though, God knows, in old days he seemed to be a very decent fellow within his limits—it's so natural that he should be going to the dogs! One must look at it from a Christian point of view! And you know, my dear, my best of friends, I want to be utterly different to him; I want to be kind to him. That would be really a 'good deed' on my part. For, you know, after all, I have wronged him! Listen, you know there's something else I must tell you. On one occasion in T—— I was in want of four thousand roubles, and he lent me the money on the spot, with no security, and showed genuine pleasure at being of use to me; and, do you know, I took it then, I took it from his hands. I borrowed money from him, do you understand, as a friend!"

"Only be more careful," Klavdia Petrovna anxiously observed, in response to all this. "And what a state of ecstasy you're in; I feel uneasy about you! Of course, Liza will be like a child of my own now. But there's so much, so much still to be settled! The great thing is that you must be more circumspect; you absolutely must be more circumspect when you are happy or so ecstatic; you're too generous when you are happy," she added, with a smile.

They all came out to see Velchaninov off. The children, who had been playing with Liza in the garden, brought her with them. They seemed to look at her with more amazement now than at first. Liza was overcome with shyness when, at parting, Velchaninov kissed her before them all, and warmly repeated his promise to come next day with her father. To the last minute she was silent and did not look at him, but then suddenly she clutched at his arm and drew him aside, fixing an imploring look on him; she wanted to tell him something. He promptly took her away into another room.

"What is it, Liza?" he asked her tenderly and reassuringly; but she, still looking about her apprehensively, drew him into the furthest corner; she wanted to be hidden from them all.

"What is it, Liza? What's the matter?"

She was dumb, she could not bring herself to speak; she gazed fixedly with her blue eyes into his face, and every feature of her little face expressed nothing but frantic terror.

"He'll . . . hang himself!" she whispered, as though in delirium.

"Who will hang himself?" asked Velchaninov in dismay.

"He, he! He tried to hang himself with a cord in the night!" the child said breathlessly. "I saw him! He tried to hang himself with a cord, he told me so, he told me so! He meant to before, he always meant to . . . I saw him in the night. . . ."

"Impossible," whispered Velchaninov in amazement.

She suddenly fell to kissing his hands; she cried, almost choking with sobs, begged and besought him, but he could make nothing of her hysterical whisperings. And the tortured face of that terror-

stricken child who looked to him as her last hope remained printed
on his memory for ever, haunting him awake and visiting his dreams.

"And can she, can she really love him so much?" he thought, jeal-
ously and enviously, as with feverish impatience he returned to town.
"She had told me herself that morning that she loved her mother
more . . . perhaps she hated him and did not love him at all! . . . And
what did that mean: he will hang himself? What did she mean by
that? Would the fool hang himself?" . . . He must find out, he must
certainly find out! He must get to the bottom of it as soon as possible—once and for all.

7. THE HUSBAND AND THE LOVER KISS EACH OTHER

He was in terrible haste "to find out."

"This morning I was so overwhelmed. This morning I hadn't the
time to realize the position," he thought, recalling his first sight of
Liza, "but now I must find out." To find out more quickly he was on
the point of telling the driver to take him to Trusotsky's lodging, but
on second thoughts decided: "No, better let him come to me, and
meanwhile I'll make haste and get this accursed legal business off my
hands."

He set to work feverishly; but this time he was conscious himself
that he was very absent-minded and that he was hardly capable that
day of attending to business. At five o'clock, when he went out to
dinner, he was struck for the first time by an absurd idea: that perhaps
he really was only hindering the progress of his case, by meddling in
the lawsuit himself, fussing about in the law-courts and hunting up his
lawyer, who was already beginning to hide from him. He laughed
gaily at his supposition. "If this idea had occurred to me yesterday, I
should have been dreadfully distressed," he added, even more gaily. In
spite of his gaiety, he grew more and more preoccupied and more and
more impatient. He fell to musing at last; and though his restless
thought clutched at one thing after another, he could arrive at nothing that would satisfy him.

"I must have that man!" he decided finally. "I must solve the riddle
of that man, and then make up my mind. It's—a duel!"

Returning home at seven o'clock, he did not find Pavel Pavlovitch
and was extremely surprised, then extremely wrathful, and later still
extremely depressed; finally he began to be actually frightened.

"God knows, God knows how it will end!" he repeated, as he

walked about the room or stretched himself on the sofa, continually looking at his watch. At last, about nine o'clock, Pavel Pavlovitch appeared. "If the fellow were trying to dupe me, he couldn't have caught me at a more favourable time—I feel so unhinged at this moment," he thought, his confidence completely restored and his spirits rising again.

To his brisk and cheerful inquiry why he was so late coming, Pavel Pavlovitch gave a wry smile, seated himself with a free and easy air, very different from his manner the night before, and carelessly threw his hat with the crape on it on another chair close by. Velchaninov at once noticed this free and easy manner and made a note of it.

Calmly, without wasting words, with none of the excitement he had shown in the morning, he told him, as though giving a report, how he had taken Liza, how kindly she had been received, how good it would be for her, and little by little, as though forgetting Liza, he imperceptibly turned the conversation entirely on the Pogoryeltsevs—what charming people they were, how long he had known them, what a splendid and influential man Pogoryeltsev was, and so on. Pavel Pavlovitch listened inattentively and from time to time glanced up from under his brows at the speaker with an ill-humoured and crafty sneer.

"You're an impulsive person," he muttered, with a particularly disagreeable smile.

"You're rather ill-humoured to-day, though," Velchaninov observed with vexation.

"And why shouldn't I be ill-humoured, like every one else!" Pavel Pavlovitch cried out suddenly, just as though he had only been waiting for that to bounce out.

"You're at liberty to please yourself," laughed Velchaninov. "I wondered if anything had happened to you."

"So it has!" the other exclaimed, as though boasting that something had happened.

"What is it?"

Pavel Pavlovitch delayed answering for a little.

"Why, our Stepan Mihalovitch has played me a trick . . . Bagautov, that elegant young Petersburg gentleman of the best society."

"Was he not at home again?"

"No, this time he was at home. For the first time I was admitted, and I gazed upon his face . . . only he was dead!"

"Wha-at! Bagautov is dead?" Velchaninov was awfully surprised, though there was no apparent reason for his being so surprised.

"Yes. For six years our true and constant friend! Only yesterday, almost at midday, he died, and I knew nothing of it! I was going maybe that very minute to inquire after his health. To-morrow there will be the service and the funeral, he's already in his coffin. The coffin is lined with crimson-coloured velvet trimmed with gold . . . he died of brain fever. I was admitted—I was admitted to gaze upon his face! I told them at the door that I was an intimate friend, that was why I was admitted. What's one to think of the way he's treated me now, my true and constant friend for six long years—I ask you that? Perhaps it was only on his account I came to Petersburg!"

"But what are you angry with him for?" laughed Velchaninov. "Why, he did not die on purpose!"

"But I speak with my heart full of regret; he was a precious friend; this was what he meant to me."

And all at once, quite unexpectedly, Pavel Pavlovitch put up his two fingers like two horns on his bald forehead and went off into a low, prolonged chuckle. He sat like that, chuckling, for a full half-minute, staring into Velchaninov's face in a frenzy of malignant insolence. The latter was petrified as though at the sight of some ghost. But his stupefaction lasted but one brief instant; a sarcastic and insolently composed smile came slowly upon his lips.

"What's the meaning of that?" he asked, carelessly drawling the words.

"The meaning of it is—horns!" Pavel Pavlovitch rapped out, taking away his fingers from his forehead at last.

"That is . . . your horns?"

"My own, generously bestowed!" Pavel Pavlovitch said with a very nasty grimace. Both were silent.

"You're a plucky fellow, I must say!" Velchaninov pronounced.

"Because I showed you my decorations? Do you know, Alexey Ivanovitch, you'd better offer me something! You know I entertained you every blessed day for a whole year at T——. Send for just one bottle, my throat is dry."

"With pleasure; you should have said so before. What will you have?"

"Why *you?* Say *we;* we'll drink together, won't we?" said Pavel Pavlovitch, gazing into his face with a challenging but at the same time strangely uneasy look.

"Champagne?"

"What else? It's not the time for vodka yet. . . ."

Velchaninov got up deliberately, rang for Mavra and gave instructions.

"To the joy of our delightful meeting after nine years' absence," said Pavel Pavlovitch, with a quite superfluous and inappropriate snig-

ger. "Now you, and you only, are the one friend left me! Stepan
Mihalovitch Bagautov is no more! As the poet says—

> "'Great Patrocus is no more,
> Vile Thersites still lives on!'"

And at the word "Thersites" he poked himself in the chest.

"You'd better hurry up and speak out, you swine; I don't like
hints," Velchaninov thought to himself. His anger was rising and for
a long time he had hardly been able to restrain himself.

"Tell me," he said in a tone of vexation, "since you accuse Stepan
Mihalovitch (he could not call him simply Bagautov now), "I should
have thought you would have been glad that the man who has
wronged you is dead; why are you angry about it?"

"Glad? Why glad?"

"I imagine those must be your feelings."

"He— he! You are quite mistaken about my feelings on that subject; as some wise man has said, 'A dead enemy is good, but a living
one is better,' he—he!"

"But you saw him living every day for five years, I believe; you had
time to get tired of the sight of him," Velchaninov observed, with
spiteful impertinence.

"But you don't suppose I knew then . . . you don't suppose I
knew?" Pavel Pavlovitch blurted out suddenly, just as though he had
bounced out from behind a corner again, and as though he were delighted to be asked a question he had long been waiting for.
"What do you take me for, then, Alexey Ivanovitch?"

And there was a gleam in his face of something quite new and unexpected, which seemed to transform his countenance, till then full of
spite and abjectly grimacing.

"Is it possible you didn't know, then?" said Velchaninov, disconcerted and completely taken by surprise.

"Is it possible I knew? Is it possible I knew? Oh, you race of
Jupiters! For you a man's no more than a dog, and you judge all ac-
cording to your own petty nature. I tell you that! You can swallow
that!" And he banged frantically on the table with his fist, but was at
once dismayed at the bang and began to look apprehensive.

Velchaninov assumed an air of dignity.

"Listen, Pavel Pavlovitch. It's absolutely nothing to me, as you can see
for yourself, whether you knew, or whether you didn't. If you didn't
know, it's to your credit in any case, though . . . I can't understand, however, why you've chosen to make this confidence to me" . . . ?

"I didn't mean you . . . don't be angry. I didn't mean you . . ." muttered Pavel Pavlovitch, looking down.

Mavra came in with the champagne.

"Here it is!" cried Pavel Pavlovitch, evidently relieved at her entrance. "Glasses, my good girl, glasses; splendid! We ask for nothing
more, my dear. And uncorked already! Honour and glory to you,
charming creature! Come, you can go!"

And with renewed courage he looked impudently at Velchaninov
again.

"Confess," he chuckled suddenly, "that all this is very interesting
and by no means 'absolutely nothing to you,' as you were pleased to
declare; so much so that you would be disappointed if I were to get
up this minute and go away without explaining myself."

"I really shouldn't be disappointed."

"Oh, that's a lie!" was what Pavel Pavlovitch's smile expressed.

"Well, let's come to business!" And he filled his glass.

"Let's drink," he pronounced, taking up the glass, "to the health of
our friend departed in God, Stepan Mihalovitch."

He raised his glass, and drank it.

"I'm not going to drink such a health," said Velchaninov, putting
down his glass.

"Why not? It's a pleasant toast."

"I say, weren't you drunk when you came in just now?"

"I had had a little. But why?"

"Nothing particular, but I thought last night, and this morning still
more, that you were genuinely grieved at the loss of Natalya
Vassilyevna."

"And who told you that I'm not genuinely grieved at the loss of
her now?" Pavel Pavlovitch bounced out again, exactly as though he
were worked by springs.

"And I didn't mean that; but you must admit that you may be mistaken about Stepan Mihalovitch, and it is—a grave matter."

Pavel Pavlovitch smiled craftily and winked.

"And wouldn't you like to know how I found out about Stepan
Mihalovitch?"

Velchaninov flushed.

"I tell you again that it's nothing to me." . . . "Hadn't I better chuck
him out this minute, bottle and all?" he thought furiously, and he
flushed a deeper crimson.

"That's all right!" said Pavel Pavlovitch, as though trying to en-
courage him, and he poured himself out another glass.

"I will explain at once how I found out all about it, and so gratify
your ardent desire . . . for you are an ardent man, Alexey Ivanovitch,
a terribly ardent man! He—he! Only give me a cigarette, for ever
since March . . . !"

"Here's a cigarette for you."

"I have gone to the dogs since March, Alexey Ivanovitch, and I'll tell you how it's all happened—listen. Consumption, as you know yourself, my best of friends," he grew more and more familiar, "is a curious disease. Consumptives have scarcely a suspicion they may be dying to-morrow and then all in a minute they're dead. I tell you that only five hours before, Natalya Vassilyevna was planning a visit a fortnight later to her aunt, thirty miles away. You are aware, too, probably, of the practice, or rather bad habit—common in many ladies and very likely in their admirers as well—of preserving all sorts of rubbish in the way of love-letters. . . . It would be much safer to put them in the stove, wouldn't it? No, every scrap of paper is carefully stored away in a box or a *nécessaire;* even docketed in years, and in months, and in series. Whether it's a comfort to them—I don't know; but, no doubt, it's for the sake of agreeable memories. Since only five hours before her end she was arranging to go to visit her aunt, Natalya Vassilyevna naturally had no thought of death to the very last hour. She was still expecting Koch. So it happened that Natalya Vassilyevna died, and an ebony box inlaid with mother-of-pearl and silver was left standing on her bureau. And it was a charming box, with a lock and key, an heirloom that had come to her from her grandmother. In that box everything lay revealed, absolutely everything; all, without exception, with the year and the day, everything for the last twenty years. And as Stepan Mihalovitch had a distinct literary bent (he actually sent a passionate love story to a journal), his contributions ran into the hundreds—to be sure they were spread out over five years. Some specimens had been annotated in Natalya Vassilyevna's own handwriting. A pleasant surprise for a husband. What do you think of it?"

Velchaninov reflected hurriedly and felt sure that he had never sent Natalya Vassilyevna a single letter, not a note of any kind. Though he had written twice from Petersburg, his letters, in accordance with a compact between them, had been addressed to the husband as well as the wife. To Natalya Vassilyevna's last letter, in which she had decreed his banishment, he had never answered.

When he had ended his story, Pavel Pavlovitch paused for a full minute with an importunate and expectant smile.

"Why do you give me no answer to my little question?" he brought out at last, with evident anxiety.

"What little question?"

"Why, the pleasant surprise for a husband on opening that box."

"Oh! what is it to do with me!" exclaimed Velchaninov, with a gesture of disgust, and he got up and walked about the room.

"And I bet you're thinking now, you're a swine to have shown me your shame. He—he! You're a very fastidious man . . . you are."

"I think nothing about it. On the contrary, you are so much exasperated by the death of the man who wronged you and you've drunk so much wine, too. I see nothing extraordinary in all this; I quite understand why you wanted Bagautov alive, and I am ready to respect your annoyance: but . . ."

"And what did I want Bagautov for, do you suppose?"

"That's your affair."

"I bet that you were thinking of a duel!"

"Damn it all!" cried Velchaninov, growing more and more unable to control himself. "I imagine that a decent man . . . in such cases does not stoop to ridiculous babble, to stupid antics, to ludicrous complaints and disgusting insinuations, by which he only degrades himself more, but acts openly, directly, straightforwardly—like a decent man!"

"He—he! but perhaps I'm not a decent man!"

"That's your affair again . . . but in that case, what the devil did you want Bagautov alive for?"

"Why, if only to see a friend. We'd have had a bottle and drunk together."

"He wouldn't have drunk with you."

"Why not? *Noblesse oblige!* Here, you're drinking with me; in what way is he better than you?"

"I haven't drunk with you."

"Why such pride all of a sudden?"

Velchaninov suddenly broke into a nervous and irritable laugh.

"Damnation! Why, you are really a 'predatory type'! I thought you were only 'the eternal husband,' and nothing more!"

"What do you mean by 'the eternal husband,' what's that?" Pavel Pavlovitch suddenly pricked up his ears.

"Oh, it's one type of husband . . . it would be a long story. You'd better clear out, it's time you were gone; I'm sick of you."

"And predatory? You said 'predatory'!"

"I said you were a 'predatory type'; I said it ironically."

"What do you mean by a 'predatory type'? Tell me, please, Alexey Ivanovitch, for God's sake, or for Christ's sake!"

"Come, that's enough, that's enough!" cried Velchaninov, suddenly growing horribly angry. "It's time you were off. Get along."

"No, it's not enough!" Pavel Pavlovitch flared up; "even though you are sick of me it's not enough, for we must drink together and clink glasses! Let us drink together, and then I'll go, but as it is it's not enough!"

"Pavel Pavlovitch! Will you go to the devil to-day or will you not?"

"I can go to the devil, but first we'll drink! You said that you would not drink *with me;* but I *want* you to drink with me!"

There was no grimacing, no sniggering about him now. He seemed all at once entirely transformed, and to have become in his whole tone and appearance so completely the opposite of the Pavel Pavlovitch of the moment before that Velchaninov was quite taken aback.

"Do let us drink, Alexey Ivanovitch! Don't refuse me," Pavel Pavlovitch persisted, gripping his hand tightly and looking strangely into his eyes.

Clearly there was more at stake than merely drinking.

"Yes, if you like," muttered Velchaninov; "but how can we? . . . There's nothing left but the dregs. . . ."

"There are just two glasses left, it's thick, but we'll drink it and clink glasses! Here, take your glass."

They clinked their glasses and emptied them.

"Since that's so—since that's so . . . Ach!"

Pavel Pavlovitch clutched his forehead in his hand and remained for some moments in that position. Velchaninov had a feeling every moment that he would speak out and utter the very *final* word. But Pavel Pavlovitch uttered nothing; he simply gazed at him and smiled again the same sly, knowing smile.

"What do you want of me, you drunken fellow! You're playing the fool with me!" Velchaninov shouted furiously, stamping.

"Don't shout, don't shout; what is there to shout for?" cried Pavel Pavlovitch, gesticulating hurriedly. "I'm not playing the fool, I'm not playing the fool! Do you know what you are to me now?"

And he suddenly seized his hand and kissed it. Velchaninov was utterly taken aback.

"That's what you mean to me now! And now—and now I'll go to the devil as soon as you please!"

"Wait a minute, stay!" cried Velchaninov, recovering himself. "I forgot to tell you. . . ."

Pavel Pavlovitch turned back from the door.

"You see," muttered Velchaninov, very quickly, flushing crimson and looking away, "you must be at the Pogoryeltsevs' to-morrow . . . to make their acquaintance and thank them; you must . . ."

"Certainly, I must. I understand that, of course!" Pavel Pavlovitch acquiesced with the utmost readiness, waving his hand quickly as though to protest that there was no need to remind him.

"And besides, Liza is very anxious to see you. I promised her . . ."

"Liza!" Pavel Pavlovitch turned back. "Liza? Do you know what

Liza has meant to me and means? Has meant and still means!" he cried all at once, almost frantically. "But . . . But of that later, all that can be later. . . . But now it's not enough that we've drunk together, Alexey Ivanovitch, I must have something else to be satisfied. . . ."

He laid his hat on a chair and gazed at him, gasping for breath a little as he had done just before.

"Kiss me, Alexey Ivanovitch!" he suggested suddenly.

"You're drunk!" Velchaninov declared, stepping back.

"Yes, but kiss me all the same, Alexey Ivanovitch. Oh, kiss me! Why, I kissed your hand just now."

For some minutes Velchaninov was silent, as though stunned by a blow on the head. But suddenly he bent down to Pavel Pavlovitch, whose face was on a level with his shoulder, and kissed him on the lips, which smelt very strongly of spirits. He was not, however, perfectly certain that he had kissed him.

"Well, now, now. . . ." Pavel Pavlovitch cried again in a drunken frenzy, his drunken eyes flashing; "now I'll tell you; I thought then, What if he too? What if that one, I thought, what if he too . . . whom can I trust after that!"

Pavel Pavlovitch suddenly burst into tears.

"So you understand, you're the one friend left me now!"

And he ran with his hat out of the room. Velchaninov again stood still for some minutes in the same place, just as he had done after Pavel Pavlovitch's first visit.

"Ah! a drunken fool and nothing more!" He waved his hand, dismissing the subject.

"Absolutely nothing more," he repeated energetically as he undressed and got into bed.

8. LIZA ILL

Next morning Velchaninov walked about his room expecting Pavel Pavlovitch, who had promised to arrive in good time to go to the Pogoryeltsevs. As he smoked and sipped his coffee he was conscious at every moment that he was like a man who on waking up in the morning cannot forget for one instant that he has received a slap in the face overnight. "H'm! . . . he quite understands the position and will take his revenge on me through Liza!" he thought with horror.

The charming figure of the poor child rose mournfully before him for a moment. His heart beat faster at the thought that he would soon, within two hours, see *his* Liza again. "Ah! it's no use talking about it!"

he decided hotly—"It's my whole life and my whole object now! what do slaps in the face or memories of the past matter? What has my life been till now? Muddle and sadness . . . but now . . . it's all different, everything's changed!"

But in spite of his enthusiasm, he grew more and more doubtful.

"He is tormenting me by means of Liza—that's clear! And he is tormenting Liza too. It's in that way he will devour me utterly in revenge for everything. H'm! . . . Of course, I can't allow him to go on as he did yesterday"—he flushed crimson all at once—"and . . . here it's twelve o'clock, though, he doesn't come."

He waited a long time, till half-past twelve, and his depression grew more and more acute. Pavel Pavlovitch did not appear. At last the thought that had long been stirring in his mind, that Pavel Pavlovitch had not come on purpose, simply in order to get up another scene like that of the night before, put the finishing touch to his irritation. "He knows that I depend on him, and what a state Liza will be in now. And how can I appear before her without him?"

At last he could stand it no longer, and at one o'clock he rushed off to the Pokrovsky Hotel alone. At the lodging he was told that Pavel Pavlovitch had not slept at home, but had only turned up at nine o'clock in the morning, had stayed no more than a quarter of an hour, and then gone out again. Velchaninov stood at the door of Pavel Pavlovitch's room, listening to what the servant said, and mechanically turned the handle of the locked door and pulled it backwards and forwards. Realizing what he was doing, he uttered a curse and asked the servant to take him to Marya Sysoevna. But the landlady, hearing he was there, came out readily.

She was a good-natured woman. "A woman with generous feelings," as Velchaninov said of her when he was reporting his conversation afterwards to Klavdia Petrovna. Inquiring briefly about his journey with the child the day before, Marya Sysoevna launched out into accounts of Pavel Pavlovitch's doings. In her words: "If it had not been for the child, she would have sent him about his business long ago. He was turned out of the hotel because of his disorderly behaviour. Wasn't it wicked to bring home a wench with him when there was a child here old enough to understand? He was shouting: 'She will be your mother, if I choose!' And, would you believe it? what that street wench did, she even spat in his face. 'You're not my daughter, but he's a ——!' she cried."

"Really!" Velchaninov was horrified.

"I heard it myself. Though the man was drunk till he was almost senseless, yet it was very wrong before the child; though she is but young, she broods over everything in her mind! The child cries. I can see she is worried to death. And the other day there was a terrible thing done in our building: a clerk, so folks say, took a room in the hotel overnight, and in the morning hanged himself. They say he had squandered all his money. People flocked to see. Pavel Pavlovitch was not at home, and the child was running about with no one to look after her; I looked, and there she was in the passage among the people, and peeping in behind the others: she was looking so strangely at the body. I brought her away as quickly as I could. And what do you think—she was all of a tremble, she looked quite black in the face, and as soon as I brought her in she flopped on the floor in a faint. She struggled and writhed, and it was all I could do to bring her round. It was a fit, and she's been poorly ever since that hour. He heard of it, came home, and pinched her all over—for he's not one for beating, he's more given to pinching her, and afterwards, when he came home after having a drop, he'd frighten her: 'I'll hang myself too,' he'd say; 'you'll make me hang myself; on this blind-cord here,' he'd say; and he'd make a noose before her eyes. And she'd be beside herself—she'd scream and throw her little arms round him: 'I won't!' she'd cry, 'I never will again.' It was pitiful."

Though Velchaninov had expected something strange, this story amazed him so much that he could not believe it.

Marya Sysoevna told him a great deal more; on one occasion, for instance, had it not been for Marya Sysoevna Liza might have thrown herself out of the window.

Velchaninov went out of the house reeling as though he were drunk.

"I'll knock him on the head like a dog!" was the thought that floated before his mind. And for a long time he kept repeating it to himself.

He took a cab and drove to the Pogoryeltsevs. On the way the carriage was obliged to stop at the cross-roads, near the bridge on the canal, over which a long funeral procession was passing. And on both sides of the bridge there were several carriages waiting in a block; people on foot were stopped too. It was a grand funeral and there was a very long string of carriages following it, and lo and behold! in the windows of one of these carriages Velchaninov caught a passing glimpse of the face of Pavel Pavlovitch. He would not have believed his eyes if Pavel Pavlovitch had not thrust his head out and nodded to him with a smile. Evidently he was delighted at recognizing Velchaninov; he even began beckoning to him from the carriage. Velchaninov jumped out of his cab and, in spite of the crush, in spite of the police, and in spite of the fact that Pavel Pavlovitch's carriage was driving on to the bridge, he ran right up to the window. Pavel Pavlovitch was alone.

"What's the matter with you?" cried Velchaninov; "why didn't you come? How is it you are here?"

"I'm repaying a debt. Don't shout, don't shout, I am repaying a debt," sniggered Pavel Pavlovitch, screwing up his eyes, jocosely. "I'm following the mortal remains of my faithful friend, Stepan Mihalovitch."

"That's all nonsense, you drunken, senseless man," Velchaninov shouted louder than ever, though he was taken aback for an instant. "Get out this minute and come into the cab with me."

"I can't, it's a duty. . . ."

"I'll drag you out!" Velchaninov yelled.

"And I'll scream! I'll scream!" said Pavel Pavlovitch, sniggering as jocosely as before, as though it were a game, though he did huddle into the furthest corner of the carriage. . . .

"Look out, look out! you'll be run over!" shouted a policeman.

At the further end of the bridge a carriage cutting across the procession did, in fact, cause a commotion. Velchaninov was forced to skip back; the stream of carriages and the crowd of people immediately carried him further away. With a curse he made his way back to the cab.

"No matter, I couldn't have taken a fellow like that with me, at any rate!" he thought, with a feeling of bewildered anxiety that persisted.

When he told Klavdia Petrovna Marya Sysoevna's story and described the strange meeting in the funeral procession, she grew very thoughtful.

"I feel afraid for you," she said. "You ought to break off all relations with him, and the sooner the better."

"He's a drunken fool and nothing more!" Velchaninov cried passionately; "as though I could be afraid of him! And how can I break off relations with him when there's Liza to be considered. Think of Liza!"

Liza meanwhile was lying ill; she had begun to be feverish the evening before and they were expecting a celebrated doctor, for whom they had sent an express messenger to the town in the morning. This completed Velchaninov's distress.

Klavdia Petrovna took him to the invalid.

"I watched her very carefully yesterday," she observed, stopping outside Liza's room. "She's a proud and reserved child; she is ashamed that she is here, and that her father has cast her off; that's the whole cause of her illness, to my thinking."

"How cast her off? Why do you say he's cast her off?"

"The very fact that he let her come here, among complete strangers and with a man . . . who's almost a stranger, too, or on such terms . . ."

"But it was I took her, I took her by force; I don't perceive . . ."

"Oh, my God, and even Liza, a child, perceives it! It's my belief that he simply won't come at all."

Liza was not astonished when she saw Velchaninov alone; she only smiled mournfully and turned her feverishly hot little head to the wall. She made no response to Velchaninov's timid efforts to comfort her and his fervent promises to bring her father next day without fail. On coming away from her, he suddenly burst into tears.

It was evening before the doctor came. After examining the patient, he alarmed them all from the first word, by observing that they had done wrong not to have sent for him before. When it was explained to him that the child had been taken ill only the evening before, he was at first incredulous.

"It all depends how things go on to-night," he said in conclusion. After giving various instructions, he went away, promising to come again next day as early as possible. Velchaninov would have insisted on staying the night, but Klavdia Petrovna begged him once more "to try and bring that monster."

"Try once more," Velchaninov retorted in a frenzy. "Why, this time I'll tie him hand and foot and carry him here in my arms!" The idea of tying Pavel Pavlovitch hand and foot and carrying him there took possession of him and made him violently impatient to carry it out. "I don't feel in the least guilty towards him now, not in the least!" he said to Klavdia Petrovna, as he said good-bye. "I take back all the abject, snivelling things I said here yesterday," he added indignantly.

Liza was lying with her eyes shut, apparently asleep; she seemed to be better. When Velchaninov cautiously bent over her head, to say good-bye and to kiss, if only the edge of her garment, she suddenly opened her eyes, as though she had been expecting him, and whispered to him—

"Take me away!"

It was a gentle, pitiful prayer, without a shade in it of the irritability of the previous day, but at the same time he could hear in it the conviction that he would not do what she asked. Velchaninov, in complete despair, began trying to persuade her that this was impossible.

In silence she closed her eyes and did not utter another word, as though she did not see or hear him.

On getting into Petersburg he told the driver to take him straight to Pokrovsky Hotel. It was ten o'clock; Pavel Pavlovitch was not in his lodging. Velchaninov spent a full half-hour in waiting for him and walking up and down the passage in sickening suspense. Marya Sysoevna assured him at last that Pavel Pavlovitch would not be back till early next morning. "Then I will come early in the morning," Velchaninov decided, and, beside himself, he set off for home.

But what was his astonishment when, at the door of his flat, he learned from Mavra that his yesterday's visitor had been waiting for him since ten o'clock.

"And has been pleased to drink tea here, and has sent out for wine again, and has given me a blue note to get it."

9. AN APPARITION

Pavel Pavlovitch had made himself exceedingly comfortable. He was sitting in the same chair as the day before, smoking a cigarette, and had just poured himself out the fourth and last glass from a bottle of wine. The teapot and an unfinished glass of tea were standing on a table close by. His flushed face was beaming with bliss. He had even taken off his coat, as it was warm, and was sitting in his waistcoat.

"Excuse me, most faithful of friends!" he cried, seeing Velchaninov and jumping up to put on his coat. "I took it off for the greater enjoyment of the moment. . . ."

Velchaninov went up to him menacingly.

"Are you not quite drunk yet? Is it still possible to talk to you?"

Pavel Pavlovitch was a little flustered.

"No, not quite. . . . I've been commemorating the deceased, but . . . not quite. . . ."

"Will you understand me too?"

"That's what I've come for, to understand you."

"Well, then; I begin by telling you straight out that you are a worthless scoundrel!" cried Velchaninov.

"If you begin like that, how will you end?" Pavel Pavlovitch protested, evidently cowed, but Velchaninov went on shouting without heeding him.

"Your daughter is dying, she is ill; have you abandoned her or not?"

"Can she really be dying?"

"She is ill, ill, exceedingly, dangerously ill!"

"Possibly some little fit . . ."

"Don't talk nonsense! She is ex—ceed—ing—ly, dangerously ill! You ought to have gone if only to . . ."

"To express my gratitude, my gratitude for their hospitality! I quite understand that! Alexey Ivanovitch, my precious, perfect friend"—he suddenly clutched Velchaninov's hand in both of his, and with drunken sentimentality, almost with tears, as though imploring forgiveness, he kept crying out: "Alexey Ivanovitch, don't shout, don't shout! Whether I die or fall drunk into the Neva—what does it matter in the real significance of things? We have plenty of time to go to Mr. Pogoryeltsev. . . ."

Velchaninov pulled himself together and restrained himself a little.

"You're drunk, and so I don't understand the sense of what you are saying," he observed sternly. "I am always ready to have things out with you, shall be glad to, in fact, as soon as possible. . . . I've come indeed. . . . But first of all I warn you that I shall take steps: you must stay the night here! To-morrow morning I'll take you and we'll go together. I won't let you go," he yelled again. "I'll tie you up and carry you there in my arms! . . . Would you like this sofa?" he said breathlessly, pointing to a wide, soft sofa, which stood opposite the one against the other wall, where he used to sleep himself.

"By all means, I can sleep anywhere. . . ."

"Not anywhere, but on that sofa! Here, take your sheets, your quilt, your pillow." All these Velchaninov took out of the cupboard and hurriedly flung them to Pavel Pavlovitch, who held out his arms submissively. "Make the bed at once, make it at once!"

Pavel Pavlovitch, loaded with his burden, stood in the middle of the room as though hesitating, with a broad drunken grin on his drunken face. But at a second menacing shout from Velchaninov he suddenly began bustling about at full speed; he pushed back the table and began, sighing and groaning, to unfold the sheets and make the bed. Velchaninov went to assist him; he was, to some extent, appeased by the alarm and submissiveness of his visitor.

"Finish your glass and go to bed," he ordered him again; he felt as though he could not help giving orders. "You sent for that wine yourself, didn't you?"

"Yes. . . . I knew you wouldn't send for any more, Alexey Ivanovitch."

"It was well you knew it, and there is something more you must know too. I tell you once more I've taken measures, I won't put up with any more of your antics, I won't put up with your drunken kisses as I did yesterday."

"I understand myself, Alexey Ivanovitch, that that was only possible once," sniggered Pavel Pavlovitch.

Hearing his answer, Velchaninov, who had been striding up and down the room, stopped almost solemnly before Pavel Pavlovitch.

"Pavel Pavlovitch, tell me frankly! You're a sensible man, I've recognized that again, but I assure you, you are on the wrong tack! Speak straightforwardly, act straightforwardly and I give you my word of honour I will answer any question you like."

Pavel Pavlovitch grinned his broad grin again, which was enough in itself to drive Velchaninov to fury.

"Stop!" Velchaninov shouted again. "Don't sham, I see through you! I repeat: I give you my word of honour, that I am ready to answer *anything* and you shall receive every satisfaction possible, that is every sort, even the impossible! Oh, how I wish you could understand me! . . ."

"Since you are so good"—Pavel Pavlovitch moved cautiously towards him—"I was much interested in what you said last night about a 'predatory type'! . . ."

Velchaninov, with a curse, fell to pacing about the room more rapidly than ever.

"No, Alexey Ivanovitch, don't curse, because I'm so much interested, and have come on purpose to make sure. . . . I'm not very ready with my tongue, but you must forgive me. You know of that 'predatory type,' and of that 'peaceable type' I read in a magazine, in the literary criticism. I remembered it this morning . . . only I had forgotten it, and to tell the truth I did not understand it at the time. This is what I wanted you to explain: the deceased, Stepan Mihalovitch Bagautov—was he 'predatory' or 'peaceable'? How do you classify him?"

Velchaninov still remained silent, and did not cease his pacing up and down.

"The predatory type," he began, stopping suddenly in exasperation, "is the man who would sooner have put poison in Bagautov's glass when drinking champagne with him in honour of their delightful meeting, as you drank with me yesterday, than have followed his coffin to the cemetery as you have to-day, the devil only knows from what secret, underground, loathsome impulse and distorted feeling that only degrades you! Yes, degrades you!"

"It's true that I shouldn't have gone," Pavel Pavlovitch assented; "but you do pitch into me. . . ."

"It's not the man," Velchaninov, getting hotter, went on shouting, without heeding him; "it's not the man who poses to himself as goodness knows what, who reckons up his score of right and wrong, goes over and over his grievance as though it were a lesson, frets, goes in for all sorts of antics and apishness, hangs on people's necks—and most likely he has been spending all his time at it too! Is it true that you tried to hang yourself—is it?"

"When I was drunk, I did talk wildly—I don't remember. It isn't quite seemly, Alexey Ivanovitch, to put poison in wine. Apart from the fact that I am a civil servant of good repute, you know I have money of my own, and, what's more, I may want to get married again."

"Besides, you'll be sent to the gallows."

"To be sure, that unpleasantness also, though nowadays they admit many extenuating circumstances in the law-courts. I'll tell you a killing little anecdote, Alexey Ivanovitch. I thought of it this morning in the carriage. I wanted to tell you of it then. You said just now 'hangs on people's necks.' You remember, perhaps, Semyon Petrovitch Livtsov, he used to come and see us when you were in T——; well, his younger brother, who was also a young Petersburg swell, was in attendance on the governor at V——, and he, too, was distinguished for various qualities. He had a quarrel with Golubenko, a colonel, in the presence of ladies and the lady of his heart, and considered himself insulted, but he swallowed the affront and concealed it; and, meanwhile, Golubenko cut him out with the lady of his heart and made her an offer. And what do you think? This Livtsov formed a genuine friendship with Golubenko, he quite made it up with him, and, what's more, insisted on being his best man, he held the wedding crown, and when they came from under the wedding crown, he went up to kiss and congratulate Golubenko; and in the presence of the governor and all the honourable company, with his swallow-tail coat, and his hair in curl, he sticks the bridegroom in the stomach with a knife—so that he rolled over! His own best man! What a disgrace! And, what's more, when he'd stabbed him like that, he rushed about crying: 'Ach! what have I done! Oh, what is it I've done!' with floods of tears, trembling all over, flinging himself on people's necks, even ladies. 'Ach, what have I done!' he kept saying. 'What have I done now!' He—he—he! he was killing. Though one feels sorry for Golubenko, perhaps, but after all he recovered."

"I don't see why you told me the story," observed Velchaninov, frowning sternly.

"Why, all because he stuck the knife in him, you know," Pavel Pavlovitch tittered; "you can see he was not the type, but a snivelling fellow, since he forgot all good manners in his horror and flung himself on the ladies' necks in the presence of the governor—but you see he stabbed him, he got his own back! That was all I meant."

"Go to hell!" Velchaninov yelled suddenly, in a voice not his own, as though something had exploded in him. "Go to hell with your underground vileness; you are nothing but underground vileness. You thought you'd scare me—you base man, torturing a child; you scoundrel, you scoundrel, you scoundrel!" he shouted, beside himself, gasping for breath at every word.

A complete revulsion came over Pavel Pavlovitch which actually seemed to sober him; his lips quivered.

"It is you, Alexey Ivanovitch, call me a scoundrel, *you* call *me?*"

But Velchaninov had already realized what he had done.

"I am ready to apologize," he answered, after a pause of gloomy hesitation; "but only if you will act straightforwardly at once yourself."

"In your place I would apologize without any ifs, Alexey Ivanovitch."

"Very good, so be it," said Velchaninov, after another slight pause. "I apologize to you; but you'll admit yourself, Pavel Pavlovitch, that, after all this, I need not consider that I owe you anything. I'm speaking with reference to the *whole* matter and not only to the present incident."

"That's all right, why consider?" Pavel Pavlovitch sniggered, though he kept his eyes on the ground.

"So much the better, then, so much the better! Finish your wine and go to bed, for I won't let you go, anyway. . . ."

"Oh, the wine. . . ." Pavel Pavlovitch seemed, as it were, a little disconcerted. He went to the table, however, and finished the last glass of wine he had poured out so long before.

Perhaps he had drunk a great deal before, for his hand trembled and he spilt part of the wine on the floor, and on his shirt and waistcoat. He finished it all, however, as though he could not bear to leave a drop, and respectfully replacing the empty glass on the table, he went submissively to his bed to undress.

"But wouldn't it be better for me not to stay the night?" he brought out for some reason, though he had taken off one boot and was holding it in his hand.

"No, it wouldn't," Velchaninov answered wrathfully, still pacing up and down the room without looking at him.

Pavel Pavlovitch undressed and got into bed. A quarter of an hour later Velchaninov went to bed too, and put out the candle.

He fell asleep uneasily. The new element that had turned up unexpectedly and complicated the whole business more than ever worried him now, and at the same time he felt that he was for some reason ashamed of his uneasiness. He was just dozing off, but he was waked up all at once by a rustling sound. He looked round at once towards Pavel Pavlovitch's bed. The room was dark (the curtains were drawn), but Velchaninov fancied that Pavel Pavlovitch was not lying down, but was sitting on the bed.

"What's the matter?" Velchaninov called to him.

"A ghost," Pavel Pavlovitch said, scarcely audibly, after a brief pause.

"What do you mean, what sort of ghost?"

"There in that room, I seem to see a ghost in the doorway."

"Whose ghost?" Velchaninov asked again, after a pause.

"Natalya Vassilyevna's."

Velchaninov stood up on the rug, and looked across the passage, into the other room, the door of which always stood open. There were only blinds instead of curtains on the window, and so it was much lighter there.

"There's nothing in that room and you are drunk. Go to bed!" said Velchaninov. He got into bed and wrapped himself in the quilt.

Pavel Pavlovitch got into bed, too, without uttering a word.

"And have you ever seen ghosts before?" Velchaninov asked suddenly, ten minutes afterwards.

Pavel Pavlovitch, too, was silent for a while.

"I thought I saw one once," he responded faintly.

Silence followed again.

Velchaninov could not have said for certain whether he had been asleep or not, but about an hour had passed when he suddenly turned round again: whether he was roused again by a rustle, he was not sure, but felt as though in the pitch-dark something white was standing over him, not quite close, but in the middle of the room. He sat up in bed and for a full minute gazed into the darkness.

"Is that you, Pavel Pavlovitch?" he said, in a failing voice.

His own voice ringing out suddenly in the stillness and the dark seemed to him somehow strange.

No answer followed, but there could be no doubt that some one was standing there.

"Is that you . . . Pavel Pavlovitch?" he repeated, more loudly—so loudly, in fact, that if Pavel Pavlovitch had been quietly asleep in his bed he would certainly have waked up and answered.

But again no answer came, yet he fancied that the white, hardly distinguishable figure moved nearer to him. Then something strange followed: something seemed to explode within him, exactly as it had that evening, and he shouted at the top of his voice, in a most hideous, frantic voice, gasping for breath at each word:

"If you . . . drunken fool . . . dare to imagine . . . that you can . . . frighten me, I'll turn over to the wall, I'll put the bedclothes over my head, and won't turn round again all night . . . to show you how much I care . . . if you were to stand there till morning . . . like a fool . . . and I spit upon you . . ."

And he spat furiously in the direction, as he supposed, of Pavel Pavlovitch, turned over to the wall, drew the bedclothes over his head as he had said and grew numb in that position, not stirring a muscle. A deathlike silence followed. Whether the phantom was moving nearer or standing still he could not tell, but his heart was beating, beating, beating violently. Fully five minutes passed, and suddenly, two steps from him, he heard the meek and plaintive voice of Pavel Pavlovitch.

"I got up, Alexey Ivanovitch, to look for the . . ." (and he mentioned a quite indispensable domestic article). "I didn't find one there. . . . I meant to look quietly under your bed."

"Why didn't you speak when I shouted?" Velchaninov asked in a breaking voice, after an interval of half a minute.

"I was frightened, you shouted so. . . . I was frightened."

"There in the corner on the left, in the little cupboard. Light the candle. . . ."

"I can do without the candle," Pavel Pavlovitch brought out meekly, making for the corner. "Forgive me, Alexey Ivanovitch, for disturbing you so. . . . I was so bewildered . . ."

But Velchaninov made no reply. He still lay with his face to the wall, and lay so all night, without once turning over. Whether it was that he wanted to do as he had said and so show his contempt—he did not know himself what he was feeling; his nervous irritability passed at last almost into delirium, and it was a long time before he went to sleep. Waking next morning between nine and ten, he jumped up and sat up in bed, as though some one had given him a shove—but Pavel Pavlovitch was not in the room—the unmade bed stood there empty; he had crept away at dawn.

"I knew it would be so," cried Velchaninov, slapping himself on the forehead.

10. IN THE CEMETERY

The doctor's fears turned out to be justified; Liza was suddenly worse—worse than Velchaninov and Klavdia Petrovna had imagined possible the evening before. Velchaninov found the invalid conscious in the morning, though she was in a high fever; afterwards he declared that she had smiled and even held out her feverish little hand to him. Whether this was really so, or whether he had imagined it, in an unconscious effort to comfort himself, he had no time to make sure; by nightfall the sick child was unconscious, and she remained so till the end. Ten days after her coming to the Pogoryeltsevs she died.

It was a sorrowful time for Velchaninov; the Pogoryeltsevs were very anxious about him. He spent those bitter days for the most part with them. During the last days of Liza's illness he would sit for whole hours together in a corner apparently thinking of nothing; Klavdia Petrovna attempted to distract his mind, but he made little response, and seemed to find it a burden even to talk to her. Klavdia Petrovna had not expected that "all this would have such an effect upon him." The children succeeded best in rousing him; in their company he sometimes even laughed, but almost every hour he would get up from his chair and go on tiptoe to look at the invalid. He sometimes fancied that she recognized him. He had no hope of her recovery, nor had any one, but he could not tear himself away from the room in which she lay dying, and usually sat in the next room.

On two occasions in the course of those days, however, he showed great activity: he roused himself and rushed off to Petersburg to the doctors, called on all the most distinguished of them, and arranged for a consultation. The second and last consultation took place the evening before Liza's death. Three days before that Klavdia Petrovna urged upon Velchaninov the necessity of seeking out M. Trusotsky: pointing out that "if the worst happened, the funeral would be impossible without him." Velchaninov mumbled in reply that he would write to him. Pogoryeltsev thereupon declared that he would undertake to find him through the police. Velchaninov did finally write a note of two lines and took it to the Pokrovsky Hotel. Pavel Pavlovitch, as usual, was not at home, and he left the letter for him with Marya Sysoevna.

At last Liza died, on a beautiful summer evening at sunset, and only then Velchaninov seemed to wake up. When they dressed the dead child in a white frock that belonged to one of Klavdia Petrovna's daughters and was kept for festivals, and laid her on the table in the drawing-room with flowers in her folded hands, he went up to Klavdia Petrovna with glittering eyes, and told her that he would bring the "murderer" at once. Refusing to listen to their advice to put off going till next day, he set off for Petersburg at once.

He knew where to find Pavel Pavlovitch; he had not only been to fetch the doctors when he went to Petersburg before. He had sometimes fancied during those days that if he brought her father to Liza, and she heard his voice, she might come to herself; so he had fallen to hunting for him like one possessed. Pavel Pavlovitch was in the same lodging as before, but it was useless for him to inquire there: "He hasn't slept here for the last three nights or been near the place," Marya Sysoevna reported; "and if he does come he's bound to be drunk, and before he's been here an hour he's off again: he's going to rack and ruin." The waiter at the Pokrovsky Hotel told Velchaninov, among other things, that Pavel Pavlovitch used to visit some young women in Voznesensky Prospect.

Velchaninov promptly looked up these young women. When he had treated them and made them presents these persons readily remembered their visitor, chiefly from the crape on his hat, after which, of course, they abused him roundly for not having been to see them again. One of them, Katya, undertook "to find Pavel Pavlovitch any time, because nowadays he was always with Mashka Prostakov, and he had no end of money, and she ought to have been Mashka Prohvostov (*i.e.* scoundrelly) instead of Prostakov (*i.e.* simple), and she'd been in the hospital, and if she (the speaker) liked she could pack the wench off to Siberia—she had only to say the word." Katya did not, however, look up Pavel Pavlovitch on that occasion, but she promised faithfully to do so another time. It was on her help that Velchaninov was reckoning now.

On reaching Petersburg at ten o'clock, he went at once to ask for her, paid the keeper to let her go, and set off to search with her. He did not know himself what he was going to do with Pavel Pavlovitch: whether he would kill him, or whether he was looking for him simply to tell him of his daughter's death and the necessity of his presence at the funeral. At first they were unsuccessful. It turned out that this Mashka had had a fight with Pavel Pavlovitch two days before, and that a cashier "had broken his head with a stool." In fact, for a long time the search was in vain, and it was only at two o'clock in the afternoon that Velchaninov, coming out of an "establishment," to which he had been sent as a likely place, unexpectedly hit up against him.

Pavel Pavlovitch, hopelessly drunk, was being conducted to this "establishment" by two ladies, one of whom was holding his arm and supporting him. They were followed by a tall, sturdy fellow, who was shouting at the top of his voice and threatening Pavel Pavlovitch with all sorts of horrors. He bawled among other things that "Pavel Pavlovitch was exploiting him and poisoning his existence." There seemed to have been some dispute about money; the women were much frightened and flustered. Seeing Velchaninov, Pavel Pavlovitch rushed to him with outstretched hands and screamed as though he were being murdered:

"Brother, defend me!"

At the sight of Velchaninov's athletic figure the bully promptly disappeared; Pavel Pavlovitch in triumph shook his fist after him with a yell of victory; at that point Velchaninov seized him by the shoulder in a fury, and, without knowing why he did it, shook him until his teeth chattered. Pavel Pavlovitch instantly ceased yelling and stared at his tormentor in stupid, drunken terror. Probably not knowing what to do with him next, Velchaninov folded him up and sat him on the curbstone.

"Liza is dead!" he said to him.

Pavel Pavlovitch, still staring at Velchaninov, sat on the curbstone supported by one of the ladies. He understood at last, and his face suddenly looked pinched.

"Dead . . ." he whispered strangely. Whether his face wore his loathsome, drunken grin, or whether it was contorted by some feeling, Velchaninov could not distinguish, but a moment later Pavel Pavlovitch, with an effort, lifted his trembling hand to make the sign of the cross; his trembling hand dropped again without completing it. A little while after he slowly got up from the curbstone, clutched at his lady and, leaning upon her, went on his way, as though oblivious— as though Velchaninov had not been present. But the latter seized him by the shoulder again.

"Do you understand, you drunken monster, that without you she can't be buried?" he shouted breathlessly.

Pavel Pavlovitch turned his head towards him.

"The artillery . . . the lieutenant . . . do you remember him?" he stammered.

"Wha—at!'" yelled Velchaninov, with a sickening pang.

"There's her father for you! Find him—for the burial."

"You're lying," Velchaninov yelled like one distraught. "You say that from spite. . . . I knew you were preparing that for me."

Beside himself, he raised his terrible fist to strike Pavel Pavlovitch. In another minute he might have killed him at one blow; the ladies squealed and were beating a retreat, but Pavel Pavlovitch did not turn a hair. His face was contorted by a frenzy of ferocious hatred.

"Do you know," he said, much more steadily, almost as though he were sober, "our Russian . . . ?" (and he uttered an absolutely unprintable term of abuse). "Well, you go to it, then!"

Then with a violent effort he tore himself out of Velchaninov's hands, stumbled and almost fell down. The ladies caught him and this time ran away, squealing and almost dragging Pavel Pavlovitch after them. Velchaninov did not follow them.

On the afternoon of the next day a very presentable-looking, middle-aged government clerk in uniform arrived at the Pogoryeltsevs' villa and politely handed Klavdia Petrovna an envelope addressed to her by Pavel Pavlovitch Trusotsky. In it was a letter enclosing three hundred roubles and the legal papers necessary for the burial. Pavel Pavlovitch wrote briefly, respectfully, and most properly. He warmly thanked Her Excellency for the kind sympathy she had shown for the little motherless girl, for which God alone could repay her. He wrote vaguely that extreme ill-health would prevent him from coming to arrange the funeral of his beloved and unhappy daughter, and he could only appeal to the angelic kindness of Her Excellency's heart. The three hundred roubles were, as he explained later in the letter, to pay for the funeral, and the expenses caused by the child's illness. If any of this money were left over he must humbly and respectfully beg that it might be spent on "a perpetual mass for the rest of the soul of the departed." The clerk who brought the letter could add nothing in explanation; it appeared, indeed, from what he said that it was only at Pavel Pavlovitch's earnest entreaty that he had undertaken to deliver the letter to Her Excellency. Pogoryeltsev was almost offended at the expression "the expenses caused by the child's illness," and after setting aside fifty roubles for the funeral— since it was impossible to prevent the father from paying for his child's burial—he proposed to send the remaining two hundred and fifty roubles back to M. Trusotsky at once. Klavdia Petrovna finally decided not to send back the two hundred and fifty roubles, but only a receipt from the cemetery church for that sum in payment for a perpetual mass for the repose of the soul of the deceased maiden Elizaveta. This receipt was afterwards given to Velchaninov to be dispatched to Pavel Pavlovitch. Velchaninov posted it to his lodging.

After the funeral he left the villa. For a whole fortnight he wandered about the town aimless and alone, so lost in thought that he stumbled against people in the street. Sometimes he would lie stretched out on his sofa for days together, forgetting the commonest things of everyday life. Several times the Pogoryeltsevs went to ask him to go to them; he promised to go, but immediately forgot. Klavdia Petrovna even went herself to see him, but did not find him at home. The same thing happened to his lawyer; the lawyer had, indeed, something to tell him: his lawsuit had been very adroitly settled and his opponents had come to an amicable arrangement, agreeing to accept an insignificant fraction of the disputed inheritance. All that remained was to obtain Velchaninov's own consent. When at last he did find him at home, the lawyer was surprised at the apathy and indifference with which Velchaninov, once such a troublesome client, listened to his explanation.

The very hottest days of July had come, but Velchaninov was oblivious of time. His grief ached in his heart like a growing abscess, and he was distinctly conscious of it and every moment with agonizing acuteness. His chief suffering was the thought that, before Liza had had time to know him, she had died, not understanding with what anguish he loved her! The object in life of which he had had such a joyful glimpse had suddenly vanished into everlasting darkness. That object—he thought of it every moment now—was that Liza should be conscious of his love every day, every hour, all her life. "No one has a higher object and no one could have," he thought sometimes, with gloomy fervour. "If there are other objects none can be holier than that!" "By my love for Liza," he mused, "all my old putrid and useless life would be purified and expiated; to make up for my own idle, vicious and wasted life I would cherish and bring up that pure and exquisite creature, and for her sake everything would be forgiven me and I could forgive myself everything."

All these *conscious* thoughts always rose before his mind, together with the vivid, ever-present and ever-poignant memory of the dead child. He re-created for himself her little pale face, remembered every expression on it: he thought of her in the coffin decked with flowers, and as she had lain unconscious in fever, with fixed and open eyes. He suddenly remembered that when she was lying on the table he had noticed one of her fingers, which had somehow turned black during her illness; this had struck him so much at the time, and he had felt so sorry for that poor little finger, that for the first time he thought of seeking out Pavel Pavlovitch and killing him; until that time he had been "as though insensible." Was it wounded pride that had tortured her wounded heart, or was it those three months of suffering at the hands of her father, whose love had suddenly changed to hatred, who had insulted her with shameful words, laughing at her terror, and had abandoned her at last to strangers? All this he dwelt upon incessantly in a thousand variations. "Do you know what Liza has been to me?"—he suddenly recalled the drunkard's exclamation and felt that that exclamation was sincere, not a pose, and that there was love in it. "How could that monster be so cruel to a child whom he had loved so much, and is it credible?" But every time he made haste to dismiss that question and, as it were, brush it aside; there was something awful in that question, something he could not bear and could not solve.

One day, scarcely conscious where he was going, he wandered into the cemetery where Liza was buried and found her little grave. He had not been to the cemetery since the funeral; he had always fancied it would be too great an agony, and had been afraid to go. But, strange to say, when he had found her little grave and kissed it, his heart felt easier. It was a fine evening, the sun was setting; all round the graves the lush green grass was growing; the bees were humming in a wild rose close by; the flowers and wreaths left by the children and Klavdia Petrovna on Liza's grave were lying there with the petals half dropping. There was a gleam of something like hope in his heart after many days.

"How serene!" he thought, feeling the stillness of the cemetery, and looking at the clear, peaceful sky.

A rush of pure, calm faith flooded his soul.

"Liza has sent me this, it's Liza speaking to me," he thought.

It was quite dark when he left the cemetery and went home. Not far from the cemetery gates, in a low-pitched wooden house on the road, there was some sort of eating-house or tavern; through the windows he could see people sitting at the tables. It suddenly seemed to him that one of them close to the window was Pavel Pavlovitch, and that he saw him, too, and was staring at him inquisitively. He walked on, and soon heard some one pursuing him; Pavel Pavlovitch was, in fact, running after him; probably he had been attracted and encouraged by Velchaninov's conciliatory expression as he watched him from the window. On overtaking him he smiled timidly, but it was not his old drunken smile; he was actually not drunk.

"Good-evening," he said.

"Good-evening," answered Velchaninov.

11. PAVEL PAVLOVITCH MEANS TO MARRY

As he responded with this "Good-evening," he was surprised at himself. It struck him as extremely strange that he met this man now without a trace of anger, and that in his feeling for him at that moment there was something quite different, and actually, indeed, a sort of impulse towards something new.

"What an agreeable evening," observed Pavel Pavlovitch, looking into his face.

"You've not gone away yet," Velchaninov observed, not by way of a question, but simply making that reflection aloud as he walked on.

"Things have dragged on, but—I've obtained a post with an increase in salary. I shall be going away the day after to-morrow for certain."

"You've got a post?" he said this time, asking a question.

"Why shouldn't I?" Pavel Pavlovitch screwed up his face.

"Oh, I only asked . . ." Velchaninov said, disclaiming the insinuation, and, with a frown, he looked askance at Pavel Pavlovitch.

To his surprise, the attire, the hat with the crape band and the whole appearance of M. Trusotsky were incomparably more presentable than they had been a fortnight before.

"What was he sitting in that tavern for?" he kept wondering.

"I was intending, Alexey Ivanovitch, to communicate with you on a subject for rejoicing," Pavel Pavlovitch began again.

"Rejoicing?"

"I'm going to get married."

"What?"

"After sorrow comes rejoicing, so it is always in life; I should be so gratified, Alexey Ivanovitch, if . . . but—I don't know, perhaps you're in a hurry now, for you appear to be . . ."

"Yes, I am in a hurry . . . and I'm unwell too."

He felt a sudden and intense desire to get rid of him; his readiness for some new feeling had vanished in a flash.

"I should have liked . . ."

Pavel Pavlovitch did not say what he would have liked; Velchaninov was silent.

"In that case it must be later on, if only we meet again . . ."

"Yes, yes, later on," Velchaninov muttered rapidly, without stopping or looking at him.

They were both silent again for a minute; Pavel Pavlovitch went on walking beside him.

"In that case, good-bye till we meet again," Pavel Pavlovitch brought out at last.

"Good-bye; I hope . . ."

Velchaninov returned home thoroughly upset again. Contact with "that man" was too much for him. As he got into bed he asked himself again: "Why was he at the cemetery?"

Next morning he made up his mind to go to the Pogoryeltsevs. He made up his mind to go reluctantly; sympathy from any one, even from the Pogoryeltsevs, was too irksome for him now. But they were so anxious about him that he felt absolutely obliged to go. He suddenly had a foreboding that he would feel horribly ashamed at their first meeting again.

Should he go or not, he thought, as he made haste to finish his breakfast; when, to his intense amazement, Pavel Pavlovitch walked in.

In spite of their meeting the day before Velchaninov could never have conceived that the man would come to see him again, and was so taken aback that he stared at him and did not know what to say. But Pavel Pavlovitch was equal to the occasion. He greeted him, and sat down on the very same chair on which he had sat on his last visit. Velchaninov had a sudden and peculiarly vivid memory of that visit, and gazed uneasily and with repulsion at his visitor.

"You're surprised?" began Pavel Pavlovitch, interpreting Velchaninov's expression.

He seemed altogether much more free and easy than on the previous day, and at the same time it could be detected that he was more nervous than he had been then. His appearance was particularly curious. M. Trusotsky was not only presentably but quite foppishly dressed—in a light summer jacket, light-coloured trousers of a smart, close-fitting cut, a light waistcoat; gloves, a gold lorgnette, which he had suddenly adopted for some reason. His linen was irreproachable; he even smelt of scent. About his whole get-up there was something ridiculous and at the same time strangely and unpleasantly suggestive.

"Of course, Alexey Ivanovitch," he went on, wriggling, "I'm surprising you by coming, and I'm sensible of it. But there is always, so I imagine, preserved between people, and to my mind there should be preserved, something higher, shouldn't there? Higher, I mean, than all the conditions and even unpleasantnesses that may come to pass. . . . Shouldn't there?"

"Pavel Pavlovitch, say what you have to say quickly, and without ceremony," said Velchaninov, frowning.

"In a couple of words," Pavel Pavlovitch began hastily, "I'm going to get married and I am just setting off to see my future bride. They are in a summer villa too. I should like to have the great honour to make bold to introduce you to the family, and have come to ask an unusual favour," (Pavel Pavlovitch bent his head humbly) "to beg you to accompany me. . . ."

"Accompany you, where?" Velchaninov stared with open eyes.

"To them, that is, to their villa. Forgive me, I am talking as though in a fever, and perhaps I've not been clear; but I'm so afraid of your declining."

And he looked plaintively at Velchaninov.

"Do you want me to go with you now to see your future bride?" Velchaninov repeated, scrutinizing him rapidly, unable to believe his eyes or ears.

"Yes," said Pavel Pavlovitch, extremely abashed. "Don't be angry, Alexey Ivanovitch. It's not impudence; I only beg you most humbly as a great favour. I had dreamed that you might not like, that being so, to refuse. . . ."

"To begin with, it's utterly out of the question." Velchaninov turned round uneasily.

"It is merely an intense desire on my part and nothing more," Pavel Pavlovitch went on, imploring him. "I will not conceal, either, that there are reasons for it, but I should have preferred not to have revealed them till later, and for the present to confine myself to the very earnest request. . . ."

And he positively got up from his seat to show his deference.

"But in any case it is quite impossible, you must admit that yourself. . . ."

Velchaninov, too, stood up.

"It is quite possible, Alexey Ivanovitch. I was proposing to present you as a friend; and besides, you are an acquaintance of theirs already; you see, it's to Zahlebinin's, to his villa. The civil councillor, Zahlebinin."

"What?" cried Velchaninov.

It was the civil councillor for whom he had been constantly looking for a month before, and had never found at home. He had, as it turned out, been acting in the interests of the other side.

"Yes, yes; yes, yes," said Pavel Pavlovitch, smiling and seeming to be greatly encouraged by Velchaninov's great astonishment; "the very man, you remember, whom you were walking beside, and talking to, while I stood opposite watching you; I was waiting to go up to him when you had finished. Twenty years ago we were in the same office, and that day, when I meant to go up to him after you had finished, I had no idea of the sort. It occurred to me suddenly, only a week ago."

"But, upon my word, they are quite a decent family," said Velchaninov, in naïve surprise.

"Well, what then, if they are?" Pavel Pavlovitch grimaced.

"No, of course, I didn't mean . . . only as far as I've observed when I was there . . ."

"They remember, they remember your being there," Pavel Pavlovitch put in joyfully; "only you couldn't have seen the family then; but he remembers you and has a great esteem for you. We talked of you with great respect."

"But when you've only been a widower three months?"

"But you see the wedding will not be at once; the wedding will be in nine or ten months, so that the year of mourning will be over. I assure you that everything is all right. To begin with, Fedosey Petrovitch has known me from a boy; he knew my late wife; he knows my style of living, and what people think of me, and what's more, I have property, and I'm receiving a post with increase of salary—so all that has weight."

"Why, is it his daughter?"

"I will tell you all about it." Pavel Pavlovitch wriggled ingratiatingly. "Allow me to light a cigarette. And you'll see her yourself today too. To begin with, such capable men as Fedosey Petrovitch are sometimes very highly thought of here in Petersburg, if they succeed in attracting notice. But you know, apart from his salary and the additional and supplementary fees, bonuses, hotel expenses, and moneys given in relief, he has nothing—that is, nothing substantial that could be called a capital. They are comfortably off, but there is no possibility of saving where there's a family. Only imagine: Fedosey Petrovitch has eight girls, and only one son, still a child. If he were to die to-morrow there would be nothing left but a niggardly pension. And eight girls! just imagine—only imagine—what it must run into simply for their shoes! Of these eight girls five are grown up, the eldest is four-and-twenty (a most charming young lady, as you will see) and the sixth, a girl of fifteen, is still at the high school. Of course, husbands must be found for the five elder ones, and that ought to be done in good time, as far as possible, so their father ought to bring them out, and what do you suppose that will cost? And then I turn up, the first suitor they have had in the house, and one they know all about, that I really have property, I mean. Well, that's all."

Pavel Pavlovitch explained with fervour.

"You're engaged to the eldest?"

"N-no, I . . . no, not to the eldest; you see, I'm proposing for the sixth, the one who is still at the high school."

"What?" said Velchaninov, with an involuntary smile. "Why, you say she's only fifteen!"

"Fifteen now; but in nine months she'll be sixteen, she'll be sixteen and three months, so what of it? But as it would be improper at present, there will be no open engagement but only an understanding with the parents. . . . I assure you that everything is all right!"

"Then it's not settled yet?"

"Yes, it is settled, it's all settled. I assure you, all is as it should be."

"And does she know?"

"Well, it's only in appearance, for the sake of propriety, that they are not telling her; of course she knows." Pavel Pavlovitch screwed up his eyes insinuatingly. "Well, do you congratulate me, Alexey Ivanovitch?" Pavel Pavlovitch concluded very timidly.

"But what should I go there for? However," he added hurriedly, "since I'm not going in any case, don't trouble to find a reason."

"Alexey Ivanovitch . . ."

"But do you expect me to get in beside you and drive off there with you? Think of it!"

The feeling of disgust and aversion came back after the momentary distraction of Pavel Pavlovitch's chatter about his future bride. In another minute he would have turned him out. He even felt angry with himself for some reason.

"Do, Alexey Ivanovitch, do, and you won't regret it!" Pavel Pavlovitch implored him in a voice fraught with feeling. "No, no, no!"—he waved his hands, catching an impatient and determined gesture from Velchaninov. "Alexey Ivanovitch, Alexey Ivanovitch, wait a bit before you decide! I see that you have perhaps misunderstood me. Of course, I know only too well that you cannot be to me, nor I to you . . . that we're not comrades; I am not so absurd as not to understand that. And that the favour I'm asking of you will not pledge you to anything in the future. And, indeed, I'm going away after to-morrow altogether, absolutely; just as though nothing had happened. Let this day be a solitary exception. I have come to you resting my hopes on the generosity of the special feelings of your heart, Alexey Ivanovitch—those feelings which might of late have been awakened . . . I think I'm speaking clearly, am I not?"

Pavel Pavlovitch's agitation reached an extreme point. Velchaninov looked at him strangely.

"You ask for some service from me?" he questioned, hesitatingly, "and are very insistent about it. That strikes me as suspicious; I should like to know more about it."

"The only service is that you should come with me. And afterwards, on our way back, I will unfold all to you as though at confession. Alexey Ivanovitch, believe me!"

But Velchaninov still refused, and the more stubbornly because he was conscious of an oppressive and malignant impulse. This evil impulse had been faintly stirring within him from the very beginning, ever since Pavel Pavlovitch had talked of his future bride: whether it was simply curiosity, or some other quite obscure prompting, he felt tempted to consent. And the more he felt tempted, the more he resisted. He sat with his elbow on one hand, and hesitated.

Pavel Pavlovitch beside him kept coaxing and persuading.

"Very good, I'll come," he consented all at once, uneasily and almost apprehensively, getting up from his seat.

Pavel Pavlovitch was extremely delighted.

"But, Alexey Ivanovitch, you must change your clothes now," Pavel Pavlovitch cajoled him, hanging gleefully about him; "put on your best suit."

"And why must he meddle in this, too, strange fellow?" Velchaninov thought to himself.

"This is not the only service I'm expecting of you, Alexey Ivanovitch. Since you have given your consent, please be my adviser."

"In what, for example?"

"The great question, for instance, of crape. Which would be more proper, to remove the crape, or keep it on?"

"As you prefer."

"No, I want you to decide; what would you do yourself in my place, that is, if you had crape on your hat? My own idea is that, if I

retain it, it points to the constancy of my feelings, and so is a flattering recommendation."

"Take it off, of course."

"Do you really think it's a matter of course?" Pavel Pavlovitch hesitated. "No, I think I had better keep it. . . ."

"As you like."

"He doesn't trust me, that's a good thing," thought Velchaninov.

They went out; Pavel Pavlovitch gazed with satisfaction at
Velchaninov's smartened appearance; his countenance seemed to betray an even greater degree of deference and of dignity! Velchaninov
wondered at him and even more at himself. A very good carriage
stood waiting for them at the gate.

"So you had a carriage all ready too? So you felt sure I should
come?"

"I engaged the carriage for myself, but I did feel confident that you
would consent to accompany me," Pavel Pavlovitch replied, with the
air of a perfectly happy man.

"Ah, Pavel Pavlovitch," Velchaninov said, laughing as it were irritably when they were in the carriage and had set off, "weren't you too
sure of me?"

"But it's not for you, Alexey Ivanovitch, it's not for you to tell me
that I'm a fool for it," Pavel Pavlovitch responded, in a voice full of
feeling.

"And Liza," thought Velchaninov, and at once hastened to dismiss
the thought of her as though afraid of sacrilege. And it suddenly
seemed to him that he was so petty, so insignificant at that moment;
it struck him that the thought that had tempted him was a thought so
small and nasty . . . and he longed again, at all costs, to fling it all up,
and to get out of the carriage at once, even if he had to thrash Pavel
Pavlovitch. But the latter began talking and the temptation mastered
his heart again.

"Alexey Ivanovitch, do you know anything about jewels?"

"What sort of jewels?"

"Diamonds."

"Yes."

"I should like to take a little present. Advise me, should I or not?"

"I think you shouldn't."

"But I feel I should so like to," returned Pavel Pavlovitch, "only,
what am I to buy? A whole set, that is, a brooch, earrings, bracelets,
or simply one article?"

"How much do you want to spend?"

"About four hundred or five hundred roubles?"

"Ough!"

"Is it too much, or what?" asked Pavel Pavlovitch in a flutter.

"Buy a single bracelet for a hundred roubles."

Pavel Pavlovitch was positively mortified; he was so eager to spend more and buy a "whole set" of jewels. He persisted. They drove to a shop. It ended, however, in his only buying a bracelet, and not the one that he wanted to, but the one that Velchaninov fixed upon. Pavel Pavlovitch wanted to take both. When the jeweller, who had asked a hundred and seventy-five roubles for the bracelet, consented to take a hundred and fifty for it, Pavel Pavlovitch was positively vexed; he would have paid two hundred if that sum had been asked, he was so eager to spend more.

"It doesn't matter, does it, my being in a hurry with presents?" he gushed blissfully, when they had set off again. "They're not grand people, they are very simple. The innocent creatures are fond of little presents," he said, with a sly and good-humoured grin. "You smiled just now, Alexey Ivanovitch, when you heard she was fifteen; but that's just what bowled me over; that she was still going to school with the satchel on her arm full of copy books and pens, he—he! That satchel fascinated me! It's innocence that charms me, Alexey Ivanovitch; it's not so much beauty of face, it's that. She giggles in the corner with her school friend, and how she laughs, my goodness! And what at? It's all because the kitten jumped off the chest of drawers on to the bed and was curled up like a little ball. . . . And then there's that scent of fresh apples! Shall I take off the crape?"

"As you please."

"I will take it off."

He took off his hat, tore off the crape and flung it in the road. Velchaninov saw that his face was beaming with the brightest hopes, as he replaced his hat upon his bald head.

"Can it be that he is really like this?" he thought, feeling genuinely angry; "can it be there isn't some trick in his inviting me? Can he be really reckoning on my generosity?" he went on, almost offended at the last supposition. "What is he—a buffoon, a fool, or the 'eternal husband'—but it's impossible!"

12. AT THE ZAHLEBININS'

The Zahlebinins were really a "very decent family," as Velchaninov had expressed it, and Zahlebinin himself had an assured position in a government office and was well thought of by his superiors. All that

Pavel Pavlovitch had said about their income was true too: "They live very comfortably, but if he dies there'll be nothing left."

Old Zahlebinin gave Velchaninov a warm and affable welcome, and his former "foe" seemed quite like a friend.

"I congratulate you, it was better so," he began at the first word, with a pleasant and dignified air. "I was in favour of settling it out of court myself and Pyotr Karlovitch (Velchaninov's lawyer) is priceless in such cases. Well, you get sixty thousand without any bother, without delay and dispute! And the case might have dragged on for three years!"

Velchaninov was at once presented to Madame Zahlebinin, an elderly lady of redundant figure, with a very simple and tired-looking face. The young ladies, too, began to sail in one after the other or in couples. But a very great many young ladies made their appearance; by degrees they gathered to the number of ten or twelve—Velchaninov lost count of them; some came in, others went out. But among them several were girl friends from the neighbouring villas. The Zahlebinins' villa, a large wooden house, built in quaint and whimsical style, with parts added at different periods, had the advantage of a big garden; but three or four other villas looked into the garden on different sides, and it was common property, an arrangement which naturally led to friendly relations among the girls of the different households. From the first words of conversation Velchaninov observed that he was expected, and that his arrival in the character of a friend of Pavel Pavlovitch, anxious to make their acquaintance, was hailed almost triumphantly.

His keen and experienced eye quickly detected something special; from the over-cordial welcome of the parents, from a certain peculiar look about the girls and their get-up (though, indeed, it was a holiday), from all that, the suspicion dawned upon him that Pavel Pavlovitch had been scheming and, very possibly, without, of course, saying it in so many words, had been suggesting a conception of him as a bachelor of property and of the "best society," who was suffering from ennui and very, very likely to make up his mind to "change his state and settle down," especially as he had just come into a fortune. The manner and the appearance of the eldest Mademoiselle Zahlebinin, Katerina Fedosyevna, the one who was twenty-four and who had been described by Pavel Pavlovitch as a charming person, struck him as being in keeping with that idea. She was distinguished from her sisters by her dress and the original way in which her luxuriant hair was done. Her sisters and the other girls all looked as though they were firmly convinced that Velchaninov was making their acquaintance "on Katya's account" and had come "to have a look at her." Their glances and even some words, dropped in the course of the day, confirmed him in this surmise. Katerina Fedosyevna was a tall blonde of generous proportions, with an exceedingly sweet face, of a gentle, unenterprising, even torpid character. "Strange that a girl like that should still be on hand," Velchaninov could not help thinking, watching her with pleasure. "Of course, she has no dowry and she'll soon grow too fat, but meantime lots of men would admire her. . . ." All the other sisters, too, were nice-looking, and among their friends there were several amusing and even pretty faces. It began to divert him; he had come, moreover, with special ideas.

Nadyezhda Fedosyevna, the sixth, the schoolgirl and Pavel Pavlovitch's bride-elect, did not appear till later. Velchaninov awaited her coming with an impatience which surprised him and made him laugh at himself. At last she made her entrance, and not without effect, accompanied by a lively, keen-witted girl friend, a brunette with a comical face whose name was Marie Nikititchna, and of whom, as was at once apparent, Pavel Pavlovitch stood in great dread. This Marie Nikititchna, a girl of twenty-three, with a mocking tongue and really clever, was a nursery governess in a friend's family. She had long been accepted by the Zahlebinins as one of themselves and was thought a great deal of by the girls. It was evident that Nadya found her indispensable now. Velchaninov discerned at once that all the girls were antagonistic to Pavel Pavlovitch, even the friends, and two minutes after Nadya's arrival he had made up his mind that she *detested* him. He observed, too, that Pavel Pavlovitch either failed to notice this or refused to.

Nadya was unquestionably the handsomest of the lot—a little brunette with a wild, untamed look and the boldness of a nihilist; a roguish imp with blazing eyes, with a charming but often malicious smile, with wonderful lips and teeth, slender and graceful, her face still childlike but glowing with the dawn of thought. Her age was evident in every step she took, in every word she uttered. It appeared afterwards that Pavel Pavlovitch did see her for the first time with an American leather satchel on her arm, but this time she had not got it.

The presentation of the bracelet was a complete failure, and, indeed, made an unpleasant impression. As soon as Pavel Pavlovitch saw his "future bride" come into the room he went up to her with a smirk. He presented it as a testimony "of the agreeable gratification he had experienced on his previous visit on the occasion of the charming song sung by Nadyezhda Fedosyevna at the piano. . . ." He stammered, could not finish, and stood helpless, holding out the case with the bracelet and thrusting it into the hand of Nadyezhda Fedosyevna, who did not want to take it, and, crimson with shame and anger, drew back her hands. She turned rudely to her mother, whose face betrayed embarassment, and said aloud:

"I don't want to take it, *maman!*"

"Take it and say thank you," said her father, with calm severity: but he, too, was displeased. "Unnecessary, quite unnecessary!" he muttered reprovingly to Pavel Pavlovitch.

Nadya, seeing there was no help for it, took the case and, dropping her eyes, curtsied, as tiny children curtsey—that is, suddenly bobbed down, and popped up again as though on springs. One of her sisters went up to look at it and Nadya handed her the case unopened, showing, for her part, that she did not care to look at it. The bracelet was taken out and passed from one to the other; but they all looked at it in silence, and some even sarcastically. Only the mother murmured that the bracelet was very charming. Pavel Pavlovitch was ready to sink into the earth.

Velchaninov came to the rescue.

He began talking, loudly and eagerly, about the first thing that occurred to him, and before five minutes were over he had gained the attention of every one in the drawing-room. He was a brilliant master of the art of small talk—that is, the art of seeming perfectly frank and at the same time appearing to consider his listeners as frank as himself. He could, with perfect naturalness, appear when necessary to be the most light-hearted and happy of men. He was very clever, too, in slipping in a witty remark, a jibe, a gay insinuation or an amusing pun, always as it were accidentally and as though unconscious of doing it—though the epigram or pun and the whole conversation, perhaps, had been prepared and rehearsed long, long before and even used on more than one previous occasion. But at the present moment nature and art were at one, he felt that he was in the mood and that something was drawing him on; he felt the most absolute confidence in himself and knew that in a few minutes all these eyes would be turned upon him, all these people would be listening only to him, talking to no one but him, and laughing only at what he said. And, in fact, the laughter soon came, by degrees the others joined in the conversation—and he was exceedingly clever in making other people talk—three or four voices could be heard at once. The bored and weary face of Madame Zahlebinin was lighted up almost with joy; it was the same with Katerina Fedosyevna, who gazed and listened as though enchanted. Nadya watched him keenly from under her brows; it was evident that she was prejudiced against him. This spurred him on the more. The "mischievous" Marie Nikititchna succeeded in getting in rather a good thrust at him; she asserted quite fictitiously that Pavel Pavlovitch had introduced him as the friend of his boyhood, so putting with obvious intent at least seven years on to his age. But even the malicious Marie Nikititchna liked him. Pavel Pavlovitch was completely nonplussed. He had, of course, some idea of his friend's abilities and at first was delighted at his success; he tittered himself and joined in the conversation; but by degrees he seemed to sink into thoughtfulness, and finally into positive dejection, which was clearly apparent in his troubled countenance.

"Well, you're a visitor who doesn't need entertaining," old Zahlebinin commented gaily, as he got up to go upstairs to his own room, where, in spite of the holiday, he had some business papers awaiting his revision; "and, only fancy, I thought of you as the most gloomy, hypochondriacal of young men. What mistakes one makes!"

They had a piano; Velchaninov asked who played, and suddenly turned to Nadya:

"I believe you sing?"

"Who told you?" Nadya snapped out.

"Pavel Pavlovitch told me just now."

"It's not true. I only sing for fun. I've no voice."

"And I've no voice either, but I sing."

"Then you'll sing to us? Well, then, I'll sing to you," said Nadya, her eyes gleaming; "only not now, but after dinner. I can't endure music," she added. "I'm sick of the piano: they're all singing and playing from morning to night here—Katya's the only one worth hearing."

Velchaninov at once took this up, and it appeared that Katerina Fedosyevna was the only one who played the piano seriously. He at once begged her to play. Every one was evidently pleased at his addressing Katya, and the mamma positively flushed crimson with gratification; Katerina Fedosyevna got up, smiling, and went to the piano, and suddenly, to her own surprise, she flushed crimson and was horribly abashed that she, such a big girl, four-and-twenty and so stout, should be blushing like a child—and all this was written clearly on her face as she sat down to play. She played something from Haydn and played it carefully though without expression, but she was shy. When she had finished Velchaninov began warmly praising to her, not her playing but Haydn, and especially the little thing which she had played, and she was evidently so pleased and listened so gratefully and happily to his praises, not of herself but of Haydn, that he could not help looking at her with more friendliness and attention: "Ah, but you are a dear!" was reflected in the gleam of his eye—and every one seemed instantly to understand that look, especially Katerina Fedosyevna herself.

"You have a delightful garden," he said, suddenly addressing the company and looking towards the glass door that led on to the balcony. "What do you say to our all going into the garden?"

"Let us, let us!" they shrieked joyfully, as though he had guessed the general wish.

They walked in the garden till dinner-time. Madame Zahlebinin, though she had been longing to have a nap, could not resist going out with them, but wisely sat down to rest on the verandah, where she at once began to doze. In the garden Velchaninov and the girls got on to still more friendly terms. He noticed that several very young men from the villas joined them; one was a student and another simply a high school boy. They promptly made a dash each for *his* girl, and it was evident that they had come on their account; the third, a very morose and dishevelled-looking youth of twenty, in huge blue spectacles, began, with a frown, whispering hurriedly with Marie Nikititchna and Nadya. He scanned Velchaninov sternly, and seemed to consider it incumbent upon himself to treat him with extraordinary contempt. Some of the girls suggested that they should play games. To Velchaninov's question, what games they played, they said all sorts of games, and catch-catch, but in the evening they would play proverbs—that is, all would sit down and one would go out, the others choose a proverb—for instance: "More haste, less speed," and when the one outside is called in, each in turn has to say one sentence to him. One, for instance, must say a sentence in which there is the word "more," the second, one in which there is the word "haste," and so on. And from their sentences he must guess the proverb.

"That must be very amusing," said Velchaninov.

"Oh, no, it's awfully boring," cried two or three voices at once.

"Or else we play at acting," Nadya observed, suddenly addressing him. "Do you see that thick tree, round which there's a seat: behind that tree is behind the scenes, and there the actors sit, say a king, a queen, a princess, a young man—just as any one likes; each one enters when he chooses and says anything that comes into his head, and that's the game."

"But that's delightful!" Velchaninov repeated again.

"Oh, no, it's awfully dull! At first it did turn out amusing, but lately it's always been senseless, for no one knows how to end it; perhaps with you, though, it will be more interesting. We did think you were a friend of Pavel Pavlovitch's, though, but it seems he was only bragging. I'm very glad you have come . . . for one thing. . . ."

She looked very earnestly and impressively at Velchaninov and at once walked away to Marie Nikititchna.

"We're going to play proverbs this evening," one of the girl friends whom Velchaninov had scarcely noticed before, and with whom he had not exchanged a word, whispered to him confidentially. "They're all going to make fun of Pavel Pavlovitch, and you will too, of course."

"Ah, how nice it is that you've come, we were all so dull," observed another girl in a friendly way. She was a red-haired girl with freckles, and a face absurdly flushed from walking and the heat. Goodness knows where she had sprung from; Velchaninov had not noticed her till then.

Pavel Pavlovitch's uneasiness grew more and more marked. In the garden Velchaninov made great friends with Nadya. She no longer looked at him from under her brows as she had at first; she seemed to have laid aside her critical attitude towards him, and laughed, skipped about, shrieked, and twice even seized him by the hand; she was extremely happy, she continued to take not the slightest notice of Pavel Pavlovitch, and behaved as though she were not aware of his existence. Velchaninov felt certain that there was an actual plot against Pavel Pavlovitch; Nadya and the crowd of girls drew Velchaninov aside, while some of the other girl friends lured Pavel Pavlovitch on various pretexts in another direction; but the latter broke away from them, and ran full speed straight to them—that is, to Velchaninov and Nadya, and suddenly thrust his bald head in between them with uneasy curiosity. He hardly attempted to restrain himself; the naïveté of his gestures and actions were sometimes amazing. He could not resist trying once more to turn Velchaninov's attention to Katerina Fedosyevna; it was clear to her now that he had not come on her account, but was much more interested in Nadya; but her expression was just as sweet and good-humoured as ever. She seemed to be happy simply at being beside them and listening to what their new visitor was saying; she, poor thing, could never keep up her share in a conversation cleverly.

"What a darling your sister Katerina Fedosyevna is!" Velchaninov said aside to Nadya.

"Katya! No one could have a kinder heart than she has. She's an angel to all of us. I adore her," the girl responded enthusiastically.

At last dinner came at five o'clock; and it was evident that the dinner, too, was not an ordinary meal, but had been prepared expressly for visitors. There were two or three very elaborate dishes, which evidently were not part of their ordinary fare, one of them so strange that no one could find a name for it. In addition to the everyday wine there was a bottle of Tokay, obviously for the benefit of the visitors; at the end of dinner champagne was brought in for some reason. Old Zahlebinin took an extra glass, became extraordinarily good-humoured and ready to laugh at anything Velchaninov said.

In the end Pavel Pavlovitch could not restrain himself. Carried away by the spirit of rivalry he suddenly attempted to make a pun too; at the end of the table, where he was sitting by Madame Zahlebinin, there was a sudden roar of loud laughter from the delighted girls.

"Papa, Papa! Pavel Pavlovitch has made a pun too," the fourth and fifth Zahlebinin girls shouted in unison. "He says we're 'damsels who dazzle all. . . .'"

"Ah, so he's punning too! Well, what was his pun?" the old man responded sedately, turning patronizingly to Pavel Pavlovitch and smiling in readiness for the expected pun.

"Why, he says we're 'damsels who dazzle all.'"

"Y-yes, well, and what then?" The old man did not understand and smiled more good-humouredly in expectation.

"Oh, Papa, how tiresome you are; you don't understand. Why, 'damsels' and then 'dazzle'; 'damsel' is like 'dazzle,' 'damsels who dazzle all. . . .'"

"A-a-ah," the old man drawled in a puzzled voice. "H'm, well, he'll make a better one next time!"

And the old man laughed good-humouredly.

"Pavel Pavlovitch, you can't have all the perfections at once," Marie Nikititchna jerked aloud. "Oh, my goodness! he's got a bone in his throat," she exclaimed, jumping up from her chair.

There was a positive hubbub, but that was just what Marie Nikititchna wanted. Pavel Pavlovitch had simply choked over the wine which he was sipping to cover his confusion, but Marie Nikititchna vowed and declared that it was a "fish bone," that she had seen it herself and that people sometimes died of it.

"Slap him on the nape of the neck," some one shouted.

"Yes, really that's the best thing to do!" the old man approved aloud.

Eager volunteers were already at him; Marie Nikititchna and the red-haired girl (who had also been invited to dinner), and, finally, the mamma herself, greatly alarmed; every one wanted to slap Pavel Pavlovitch on the back. Jumping up from the table, Pavel Pavlovitch wriggled away and was for a full minute asseverating that he had swallowed his wine too quickly and that the cough would soon be over, while the others realized that it was all a trick of Marie Nikititchna's.

"But, really, you tease . . . !" Madame Zahlebinin tried to say sternly to Marie Nikititchna: but she broke down and laughed as she very rarely did, and that made quite a sensation of a sort.

After dinner they all went out on the verandah to drink coffee.

"And what lovely days we're having!" said the old man, looking with pleasure into the garden, and serenely admiring the beauties of nature. "If only we could have some rain. Enjoy yourselves and God bless you! And you enjoy yourself too," he added, patting Pavel Pavlovitch on the shoulder as he went out.

When they had all gone out into the garden again, Pavel Pavlovitch suddenly ran up to Velchaninov and pulled him by the sleeve.

"Just one minute," he whispered impatiently.

They turned into a lonely side path.

"No, in this case, excuse me, no, I won't give up . . ." he stuttered in a furious whisper, clutching Velchaninov's arm.

"What? what?" Velchaninov asked, opening his eyes in amazement.

Pavel Pavlovitch stared at him mutely, his lips moved, and he smiled furiously.

"Where are you going? Where are you? Everything's ready," they heard the ringing, impatient voices of the girls.

Velchaninov shrugged his shoulders and returned to the rest of the party.

Pavel Pavlovitch, too, ran after him.

"I'll bet he asked you for a handkerchief," said Marie Nikititchna; "he forgot one last time too."

"He'll always forget it!" the fifth Zahlebinin girl put in.

"He's forgotten his handkerchief, Pavel Pavlovitch has forgotten his handkerchief, Mamma, Pavel Pavlovitch has forgotten his pocket-handkerchief, Mamma, Pavel Pavlovitch has a cold in his head again!" cried voices.

"Then why doesn't he say so! You do stand on ceremony, Pavel Pavlovitch!" Madame Zahlebinin drawled in a sing-song voice. "It's dangerous to trifle with a cold; I'll send you a handkerchief directly. And why has he always got a cold in his head?" she added, as she moved away, glad of an excuse for returning home.

"I have two pocket-handkerchiefs and I haven't a cold in my head!" Pavel Pavlovitch called after her, but the lady apparently did not grasp what he said, and a minute later, when Pavel Pavlovitch was ambling after the others, keeping near Velchaninov and Nadya, a breathless maid-servant overtook him and brought him a handkerchief.

"Proverbs, a game of proverbs," the girls shouted on all sides, as though they expected something wonderful from "a game of proverbs."

They fixed on a place and sat down on a seat; it fell to Marie Nikititchna's lot to guess; they insisted that she should go as far away as possible and not listen; in her absence they chose a proverb and distributed the words. Marie Nikititchna returned and guessed the proverb at once. The proverb was: "It is no use meeting troubles half-way."

Marie Nikititchna was followed by the young man with dishevelled hair and blue spectacles. They insisted on even greater precautions with him—he had to stand in the arbour and keep his face to the fence. The gloomy young man did what was required of him contemptuously, and seemed to feel morally degraded by it. When he was called he could guess nothing, he went the round of all of them and listened to what they said twice over, spent a long time in gloomy meditation, but nothing came of it. They put him to shame. The proverb was: "To pray to God and serve the Czar ne'er fail of their reward."

"And the proverb's disgusting!" the exasperated young man exclaimed indignantly, as he retreated to his place.

"Oh, how dull it is!" cried voices.

Velchaninov went out; he was hidden even further off; he, too, failed to guess.

"Oh, how dull it is!" more voices cried.

"Well, now, I'll go out," said Nadya.

"No, no, let Pavel Pavlovitch go out now, it's Pavel Pavlovitch's turn," they all shouted, growing more animated.

Pavel Pavlovitch was led away, right up to the fence in the very corner, and made to stand facing it, and that he might not look round, the red-haired girl was sent to keep watch on him. Pavel Pavlovitch, who had regained his confidence and almost his cheerfulness, was determined to do his duty properly and stood stock-still, gazing at the fence and not daring to turn round. The red-haired girl stood on guard twenty paces behind him nearer to the party in the arbour, and she exchanged signals with the girls in some excitement; it was evident that all were expecting something with trepidation; something was on foot. Suddenly the red-haired girl waved her arms as a signal to the arbour. Instantly they all jumped up and ran off at breakneck speed.

"Run, you run, too," a dozen voices whispered to Velchaninov, almost with horror at his not running.

"What's the matter? What has happened?" he asked, hurrying after them.

"Hush, don't shout! Let him stand there staring at the fence while we all run away. See, Nastya is running."

The red-haired girl (Nastya) was running at breakneck speed, waving her hands as though something extraordinary had happened. They all ran at last to the other side of the pond, the very opposite corner of the garden. When Velchaninov had got there he saw that Katerina Fedosyevna was hotly disputing with the others, especially with Nadya and Marie Nikititchna.

"Katya, darling, don't be angry!" said Nadya, kissing her.

"Very well, I won't tell Mamma, but I shall go away myself, for it's very horrid. What must he be feeling at the fence there, poor man!"

She went away—from pity—but all the others were merciless and as ruthless as before. They all insisted sternly that when Pavel Pavlovitch came back, Velchaninov should take no notice of him, as though nothing had happened.

"And let us all play catch-catch!" cried the red-haired girl ecstatically.

It was at least a quarter of an hour before Pavel Pavlovitch rejoined the party. For two-thirds of that time he had certainly been standing at the fence. The game was in full swing, and was a great success—everybody was shouting and merry. Frantic with rage, Pavel Pavlovitch went straight up to Velchaninov and pulled at his sleeve again.

"Just half a minute!"

"Good gracious, what does he want with his half-minutes!"

"He's borrowing a handkerchief again," was shouted after him once more.

"Well, this time it was you; now it's all your doing. . . ."

Pavel Pavlovitch's teeth chattered as he said this.

Velchaninov interrupted him, and mildly advised him to be livelier, or they would go on teasing him. "They tease you because you are cross when all the rest are enjoying themselves." To his surprise, these words of advice made a great impression on Pavel Pavlovitch; he subsided at once—so much so, in fact, that he went back to the party with a penitent air and submissively took his place in the game; after which they left him alone and treated him like the rest—and before half an hour had passed he had almost regained his spirits. In all the games when he had to choose a partner he picked out by preference the red-haired traitress, or one of the Zahlebinin sisters. But to his still greater surprise Velchaninov noticed that Pavel Pavlovitch did not dare try to speak to Nadya, although he continually hovered about her. At any rate he accepted his position, as an object of scorn and neglect to her, as though it were a fitting and natural thing. But towards the end they played a prank upon him again.

The game was "hide-and-seek." The one who hid, however, was allowed to run anywhere in the part of the garden allotted him. Pavel Pavlovitch, who had succeeded in concealing himself completely in some thick bushes, conceived the idea of running out and making a bolt for the house. He was seen and shouts were raised; he crept hurriedly upstairs to the first floor, knowing of a place behind a chest of drawers where he could hide. But the red-haired girl flew up after him, crept on tiptoe to the door and turned the key on him. All left off playing and ran just as they had done before to the other side of

the pond, at the further end of the garden. Ten minutes later, Pavel
Pavlovitch, becoming aware that no one was looking for him, peeped
out of the window. There was no one to be seen. He did not dare to
call out for fear of waking the parents; the maids had been sternly forbidden to answer Pavel Pavlovitch's call or go to him. Katerina
Fedosyevna might have unlocked him, but, returning to her room and
sitting down to dream a little, she had unexpectedly fallen asleep too.
And so he stayed there about an hour. At last the girls came, as it were
by chance, in twos and threes.

"Pavel Pavlovitch, why didn't you come out to us? Oh, it has been
fun! We've been playing at acting. Alexey Ivanovitch has been acting
'a young man.'"

"Pavel Pavlovitch, why don't you come, we want to admire you!"
others observed as they passed.

"Admire what now?" they suddenly heard the voice of Madame
Zahlebinin, who had only just woken up and made up her mind to
come out into the garden and watch the "children's" games while
waiting for tea.

"But here's Pavel Pavlovitch," they told her, pointing to the window where Pavel Pavlovitch's face, pale with anger, looked out with a
wry smile.

"It's an odd fancy for a man to sit alone, when you're all enjoying
yourselves!" said the mamma, shaking her head.

Meanwhile, Nadya had deigned to give Velchaninov an explanation of her words that she "was glad he had come for one reason."

The explanation took place in a secluded avenue. Marie
Nikititchna purposely summoned Velchaninov, who was taking part
in some game and was horribly bored, and left him alone in the avenue with Nadya.

"I am absolutely convinced," she said boldly, in a rapid patter, "that
you are not such a great friend of Pavel Pavlovitch's as he boasted you
were. I am reckoning on you as the one person who can do me a very
great service." She took the case out of her pocket. "I humbly beg you
to give this back to him at once, as I shall never speak to him again in
my life. You can say so from me, and tell him not to dare to force his
company and his presents on me. I'll let him know the rest through
other people. Will you be so kind as to do what I want?"

"Oh, for mercy's sake, spare me!" Velchaninov almost cried out,
waving his hand.

"What? Spare you?" Nadya was extraordinarily surprised at his re-
fusal, and she gazed at him round-eyed.

The tone she had assumed for the occasion broke down immediately, and she was almost in tears.

Velchaninov laughed.

"I don't mean that.... I should be very glad ... but I have my own account to settle with him. ..."

"I knew that you were not his friend and that he was telling lies!" Nadya interrupted quickly and passionately. "I'll never marry him, I tell you! Never! I can't understand how he could presume ... Only you must give him back his disgusting present or else what shall I do? I particularly, particularly want him to have it back to-day, the same day, so that his hopes may be crushed, and if he sneaks about it to Papa he shall see what he gets by it."

And from behind the bushes there suddenly emerged the young man in the blue spectacles.

"It's your duty to return the bracelet," he blurted out furiously, pouncing on Velchaninov. "If only from respect for the rights of women, that is—if you are capable of rising to the full significance of the question."

But before he had time to finish Nadya tugged at his sleeve with all her might, and drew him away from Velchaninov.

"My goodness, how silly you are, Predposylov!" she cried. "Go away, go away, go away, and don't dare to listen; I told you to stand a long way off!" ... She stamped her little foot at him, and when he had crept back into the bushes she still walked up and down across the path, with her eyes flashing and her arms folded before her, as though she were beside herself with anger.

"You wouldn't believe how silly they are!" She stopped suddenly before Velchaninov. "It amuses you, but think what it means to me."

"That's not *he*, it's not *he*, is it?" laughed Velchaninov.

"Of course it isn't, and how could you imagine it!" cried Nadya, smiling and blushing. "That's only his friend. But I can't understand the friends he chooses; they all say that he's a 'future leader,' but I don't understand it.... Alexey Ivanovitch, I've no one I can appeal to; I ask you for the last time, will you give it back?"

"Oh, very well, I will; give it me."

"Ah, you are kind, you are good!" she cried, delighted, handing him the case. "I'll sing to you the whole evening for that, for I sing beautifully, do you know. I told you a fib when I said I didn't like music. Oh, you must come again—once at any rate; how glad I should be. I would tell you everything, everything, everything, and a great deal more besides, because you're so kind—as kind, as kind, as—as Katya!"

And when they went in to tea she did sing him two songs, in an utterly untrained and hardly mature, but pleasant and powerful voice. When they came in from the garden Pavel Pavlovitch was stolidly sitting with the parents at the tea-table, on which the big family samovar

was already boiling, surrounded by cups of Sèvres china. He was probably discussing very grave matters with the old people, as two days
later he was going away for nine whole months. He did not glance at
the party as they came in from the garden, and particularly avoided
looking at Velchaninov. It was evident, too, that he had not been
sneaking and that all was serene so far.

But when Nadya began singing he put himself forward at once.
Nadya purposely ignored one direct question he addressed her, but
this did not disconcert Pavel Pavlovitch, or make him hesitate. He
stood behind her chair and his whole manner showed that this was his
place and he was not going to give it up to any one.

"Alexey Ivanovitch sings, Mamma; Alexey Ivanovitch wants to
sing, Mamma!" almost all the girls shouted at once, crowding round
the piano at which Velchaninov confidently installed himself, intending to play his own accompaniment. The old people came in, and
with them Katerina Fedosyevna, who had been sitting with them,
pouring out the tea.

Velchaninov chose a song of Glinka's, now familiar to almost every
one—

> "In the glad hour when from thy lips
> Come murmurs tender as a dove's."

He sang it, addressing himself entirely to Nadya, who was standing at his elbow nearer to him than any one. His voice had passed
its prime, but what was left of it showed that it had once been a
fine one. Velchaninov had, twenty years before, when he was a student, the luck to hear that song for the first time sung by Glinka
himself, at the house of a friend of the composer's. It was at a literary and artistic bachelor gathering, and Glinka, growing expan-
sive, played and sang his own favourite compositions, among them
this song. He, too, had little voice left then, but Velchaninov remembered the great impression made by that song. A drawing-
room singer, however skilful, would never have produced such an
effect. In that song the intensity of passion rises, mounting higher
and higher at every line, at every word; and, from this very intensity, the least trace of falsity, of exaggeration or unreality, such as
passes muster so easily at an opera, would distort and destroy the
whole value of it. To sing that slight but exceptional song it was
essential to have truth, essential to have real inspiration, real passion, or a complete poetical comprehension of it. Otherwise the
song would not only be a failure but might even appear unseemly
and almost shameless: without them it would be impossible to express such intensity of passion without arousing repulsion, but

truth and simplicity saved it. Velchaninov remembered that he had
made a success with this song on some occasion. He had almost re-
produced Glinka's manner of singing, but now, from the first note,
from the first line, there was a gleam of inspiration in his singing
which quivered in his voice.

At every word the torrent of feeling was more fervent and more
boldly displayed; in the last lines the cry of passion is heard, and when,
with blazing eyes, Velchaninov addressed the last words of the song to
Nadya—

> "Grown bolder, in thine eyes I gaze;
> Draw close my lips, can hear no more,
> I long to kiss thee, kiss thee, kiss thee!
> I long to kiss thee, kiss thee, kiss thee!"—

she trembled almost with alarm, and even stepped back; the colour
rushed into her cheeks, and at the same time Velchaninov seemed to
catch a glimpse of something responsive in her abashed and almost
dismayed little face. The faces of all the audience betrayed their en-
chantment and also their amazement: all seemed to feel that it was disgraceful and impossible to sing like that, and yet at the same time all
their faces were flushed and all their eyes glowed and seemed to be
expecting something more. Among those faces Velchaninov had a vision especially of the face of Katerina Fedosyevna, which looked almost beautiful.

"What a song," old Zahlebinin muttered, a little flabbergasted; "but
. . . isn't it too strong? charming, but strong. . . ."

"Yes . . ." Madame Zahlebinin chimed in, but Pavel Pavlovitch
would not let her go on; he dashed forward suddenly like one possessed, so far forgetting himself as to seize Nadya by the arm and pull
her away from Velchaninov; he skipped up to him, gazed at him with
a desperate face and quivering lips that moved without uttering a
sound.

"Half a minute," he uttered faintly at last.

Velchaninov saw that in another minute the man might be guilty of
something ten times as absurd; he made haste to take his arm and, re-
gardless of the general amazement, drew him out into the verandah,
and even took some steps into the garden with him, where it was now
almost dark.

"Do you understand that you must go away with me this minute?"
said Pavel Pavlovitch.

"No, I don't understand. . . ."

"Do you remember," Pavel Pavlovitch went on, in his frenzied
whisper, "do you remember that you insisted that I should tell you

everything, *everything* openly, 'the very last word . . .' do you remember? Well, the time has come to say that word . . . let us go!"

Velchaninov thought a minute, looked at Pavel Pavlovitch and agreed to go.

The sudden announcement of their departure upset the parents, and made all the girls horribly indignant.

"At least have another cup of tea," said Madame Zahlebinin plaintively.

"Come, what's upset you?" old Zahlebinin said in a tone of severity and displeasure, addressing Pavel Pavlovitch, who stood simpering and silent.

"Pavel Pavlovitch, why are you taking Alexey Ivanovitch away?" the girls began plaintively, looking at him with exasperation.

Nadya gazed at him so wrathfully that he positively squirmed, but he did not give way.

"You see, Pavel Pavlovitch has reminded me—many thanks to him for it—of a very important engagement which I might have missed," Velchaninov said, smiling, as he shook hands with Zahlebinin, and bowed to the mamma and the girls, especially distinguishing Katerina Fedosyevna in a manner apparent to all.

"We are very grateful for your visit and shall always be glad to see you," Zahlebinin said ponderously, in conclusion.

"Ah, we shall be so delighted . . ." the mamma chimed in with feeling.

"Come again, Alexey Ivanovitch, come again!" numerous voices were heard calling from the verandah, when he had already got into the carriage with Pavel Pavlovitch; there was perhaps one voice that called more softly than the others, "Come again, dear, dear Alexey Ivanovitch."

"That's the red-haired girl," thought Velchaninov.

13. ON WHOSE SIDE MOST?

He might think about the red-haired girl, and yet his soul was in agonies of vexation and remorse. And, indeed, during the whole of that day, which seemed on the surface so amusingly spent, a feeling of acute depression had scarcely left him. Before singing the song he did not know how to get away from it; perhaps that was why he had sung it with such fervour.

"And I could demean myself like that . . . tear myself away from everything," he began reproaching himself, but he hurriedly cut short his thoughts. Indeed, it seemed to him humiliating to lament; it was a great deal more pleasant to be angry with some one.

"Fool!" he whispered wrathfully, with a side glance at the silent figure of Pavel Pavlovitch sitting beside him in the carriage.

Pavel Pavlovitch remained obstinately silent, perhaps concentrated on preparing what he had got to say. With an impatient gesture he sometimes took off his hat and wiped his brow with his handkerchief.

"Perspiring!" Velchaninov thought spitefully.

On one occasion only Pavel Pavlovitch addressed a question to the coachman. "Is there going to be a storm?" he asked.

"Storm, indeed! Not a doubt of it; it's been brewing up all day."

The sky was indeed growing dark and there were flashes of lightning in the distance.

They reached the town about half-past ten.

"I am coming in with you, of course," Pavel Pavlovitch warned him, not far from the house.

"I understand, but I must tell you that I feel seriously unwell."

"I won't stay, I won't stay long."

When they went in at the gate, Pavel Pavlovitch ran in at the porter's lodge to find Mavra.

"What were you running off there for?" Velchaninov said sternly, as the latter overtook him and they went into the room.

"Oh . . . nothing . . . the driver . . ."

"I won't have you drink!"

No answer followed. Velchaninov lighted the candle, and Pavel Pavlovitch at once sat down on the chair. Velchaninov remained standing before him, with a frown on his face.

"I, too, promised to say my 'last' word," he began, with an inward, still suppressed irritation. "Here it is—that word: I consider on my conscience that everything between us is over, so that, in fact, there is nothing for us to talk about—do you hear?—nothing; and so wouldn't it be better for you to go away at once, and I'll close the door after you?"

"Let us settle our account, Alexey Ivanovitch," said Pavel Pavlovitch, looking in his face, however, with peculiar mildness.

"Set-tle our ac-count!" repeated Velchaninov, greatly surprised. "That's a strange thing to say! Settle what account? Bah! Isn't that perhaps that 'last word' you promised . . . to reveal to me?"

"It is."

"We've no account to settle; we settled our account long ago!" Velchaninov pronounced proudly.

"Can you really think so?" Pavel Pavlovitch brought out in a voice full of feeling, clasping his hands strangely and holding them before his breast.

Velchaninov made him no answer, but continued pacing up and down the room. "Liza! Liza!" he was moaning in his heart.

"What did you want to settle, though?" he asked him, frowning, after a rather prolonged silence.

Pavel Pavlovitch had been following him about the room with his eyes all this time, still holding his hands clasped before him.

"Don't go there again," he almost whispered in a voice of entreaty, and he suddenly got up from his chair.

"What! So that's all you are thinking about?" Velchaninov laughed spitefully. "You've surprised me all day, though!" he was beginning malignantly, but suddenly his whole face changed. "Listen," he said mournfully, with deep and sincere feeling; "I consider that I have never lowered myself as I have to-day—to begin with, by consenting to go with you, and then—by what happened there. . . . It was so paltry, so pitiful. . . . I've defiled and debased myself by mixing myself up in it . . . and forgetting . . . But there!" he cried hastily. "Listen, you attacked me to-day in an unguarded moment when I was nervous and ill . . . but there's no need to justify myself! I'm not going there again, and I assure you I take no interest in them whatever," he concluded resolutely.

"Really, really?" cried Pavel Pavlovitch, not disguising his relief and excitement.

Velchaninov looked at him contemptuously, and began pacing up and down the room again.

"You seem to have made up your mind to be happy?" he could not refrain from observing.

"Yes," Pavel Pavlovitch repeated naïvely, in a low voice.

"What is it to me," Velchaninov reflected, "that he's a buffoon and only spiteful through stupidity? I can't help hating him, though he isn't worth it!"

"I am 'the eternal husband'!" said Pavel Pavlovitch, with an abjectly submissive smile at his own expense. "I heard that expression from you, Alexey Ivanovitch, long ago, when you were staying with us in those days. I remember a great many of your sayings in that year. Last time, when you said here, 'the eternal husband,' I reflected."

Mavra came in with a bottle of champagne and two glasses.

"Forgive me, Alexey Ivanovitch; you know that I can't get on without it! Don't think it's impudence; look upon me as an outsider not on your level."

"Yes . . ." Velchaninov muttered with repugnance, "but I assure you I feel unwell. . . ."

"Directly . . . directly . . . in one minute," said Pavel Pavlovitch fussily; "just one little glass because my throat . . ."

He greedily tossed off a glassful at a gulp and sat down, looking almost tenderly at Velchaninov.

Mavra went out.

"How beastly!" Velchaninov murmured.

"It's only those girl friends," Pavel Pavlovitch said confidently, all of a sudden completely revived.

"What? Ah, yes, you are still at that. . . ."

"It's only those girl friends! And then she's so young; we have our little airs and graces! They're charming, in fact. But then—then, you know, I shall be her slave; when she's treated with deference, when she sees something of society . . . she'll be transformed."

"I shall have to give him back that bracelet, though," thought Velchaninov, scowling, as he felt the case in his pocket.

"You say that I'm resolved to be happy? I must get married, Alexey Ivanovitch," Pavel Pavlovitch went on confidentially and almost touchingly, "or what will become of me? You see for yourself!" He pointed to the bottle. "And that's only one-hundredth of my vices. I can't get on at all without marriage and—without new faith; I shall have faith and shall rise up again."

"But why on earth do you tell me this?" Velchaninov asked, almost bursting with laughter. It all struck him as wild. "But tell me," he cried, "what was your object in dragging me out there? What did you want me there for?"

"As a test . . ." Pavel Pavlovitch seemed suddenly embarrassed.

"A test of what?"

"The effect. . . . You see, Alexey Ivanovitch, it's only a week altogether . . . I've been looking round there." (Pavel Pavlovitch grew more and more confused.) "Yesterday I met you and thought: 'I've never yet seen her in outside, so to say, society, that is, in men's, except my own. . . .' A stupid idea; I feel that myself now; unnecessary. I expected too much . . . it's my horrible character. . . ."

He suddenly raised his head and flushed crimson.

"Can he be telling the whole truth?" Velchaninov was petrified with surprise.

"Well, and what then?" he asked.

Pavel Pavlovitch gave a sugary and, as it were, crafty smile.

"It's only charming childishness! It's all those girl friends! Only forgive me for my stupid behaviour before you to-day, Alexey Ivanovitch; I never will again; and indeed it will never happen again."

"And I shan't be there again," said Velchaninov, with a smile.

"That's partly what I mean."

Velchaninov felt a little piqued.

"But I'm not the only man in the world, you know," he observed irritably.

Pavel Pavlovitch flushed again.

"It's sad for me to hear that, Alexey Ivanovitch, and, believe me, I've such a respect for Nadyezhda Fedosyevna ..."

"Excuse me, excuse me, I didn't mean anything; it only seems a little strange to me that you have such an exaggerated idea of my attractions ... and ... such genuine confidence in me."

"I had such confidence just because it was after all ... that happened in the past."

"Then if so, you look upon me even now as a most honourable man?" said Velchaninov, suddenly halting.

At another time he would have been horrified at the naïveté of his own question.

"I always thought you so," said Pavel Pavlovitch, dropping his eyes.

"Why, of course. . . . I didn't mean that; that is, not in that sense. I only meant to say that, in spite of any ... preconceptions ..."

"Yes, in spite of preconceptions."

"When you came to Petersburg?" Velchaninov could not resist asking, though he felt how utterly monstrous was his curiosity.

"When I came to Petersburg, too, I looked upon you as the most honourable of men. I always respected you, Alexey Ivanovitch."

Pavel Pavlovitch raised his eyes and looked candidly, without a trace of embarrassment, at his opponent. Velchaninov was suddenly panic-stricken; he was not at all anxious that anything should happen, or that anything should overstep a certain line, especially as he had provoked it.

"I loved you, Alexey Ivanovitch," Pavel Pavlovitch articulated, as though he had suddenly made up his mind to speak, "and all that year at T—— I loved you. You did not notice it," he went on, in a voice that quivered, to Velchaninov's positive horror; "I was too insignificant, compared with you, to let you see it. And there was no need, indeed, perhaps. And I've thought of you all these nine years, because there has never been another year in my life like that one." (Pavel Pavlovitch's eyes began to glisten.) "I remembered many of your phrases and sayings, your thoughts. I always thought of you as a man with a passion for every noble feeling, a man of education, of the highest education and of ideas: 'Great ideas spring not so much from noble intelligence as from noble feeling.' You said that yourself; perhaps you've forgotten it, but I remembered it. I always looked on you, therefore, as a man of noble feeling ... and therefore believed in you—in spite of anything ..."

His chin suddenly began quivering. Velchaninov was in absolute terror; this unexpected tone must be cut short at all costs.

"That's enough, Pavel Pavlovitch, please," he muttered, flushing and irritably impatient. "And why," he screamed suddenly, "why do you fasten upon a man when he is nervous and ill, when he is almost delirious, and drag him into this darkness . . . when it's . . . when it's—nothing but delusion, mirage, and falsity, and shameful, and unnatural, and—exaggerated—and that's what's worst, that's what's most shameful—that it is so exaggerated! And it's all nonsense; we are both vicious, underground, loathsome people. . . . And if you like I'll prove that you don't like me at all, but hate me with all your might, and that you're lying, though you don't know it; you insisted on taking me there, not with the absurd object of testing your future bride (what an idea!); you saw me yesterday and felt *vindictive,* and took me there to show me and say to me, 'See what a prize! She will be mine; do your worst now!' You challenged me, perhaps you didn't know it yourself; that's how it was, for that's what you were feeling . . . and without hating me you couldn't have challenged me like that; and so you hate me!"

He rushed about the room as he shouted this. What harassed and mortified him most of all was the humiliating consciousness that he was demeaning himself so far to Pavel Pavlovitch.

"I wanted to be reconciled with you, Alexey Ivanovitch!" the other articulated suddenly, in a rapid whisper, and his chin began twitching again.

Velchaninov was overcome by furious rage, as though no one had ever insulted him so much.

"I tell you again," he yelled, "that you're fastening upon a man who's nervous and ill . . . that you're fastening upon him to extort something monstrous from him in delirium! We . . . we are men of different worlds, understand that, and . . . and . . . between us lies a grave!" he added in a furious whisper, and suddenly realized what he had done. . . .

"And how do you know"—Pavel Pavlovitch's face was suddenly pale and distorted—"how do you know what that little grave here means . . . for me!" he cried, stepping up to Velchaninov with a ridiculous but horrible gesture, pressed his fist against his heart. "I know that little grave here, and we both stand at the side of that little grave, but on my side there is more than on yours, more . . ." he whispered as though in delirium, still thumping at his heart with his fist, "more, more, more . . ."

Suddenly an extraordinarily loud ring at the door brought both of them to their senses. The bell rang so violently that it seemed as though some one had vowed to break it at the first pull.

"People don't ring like that to see me," said Velchaninov in perplexity.

"Nor to see me either," Pavel Pavlovitch whispered timidly, recovering himself too, and at once turning into the old Pavel Pavlovitch again.

Velchaninov scowled and went to open the door.

"M. Velchaninov, if I'm not mistaken?" they heard in a ringing, youthful, and exceptionally self-confident voice in the passage.

"What is it?"

"I have trustworthy information," continued the ringing voice, "that a certain Trusotsky is with you at this moment. I must see him instantly."

It would certainly have pleased Velchaninov at that moment to have given the self-confident young gentleman a vigorous kick and to have sent him flying out on the stairs; but he thought a moment, moved aside and let him in.

"Here is M. Trusotsky; come in. . . ."

14. SASHENKA AND NADENKA

There walked into the room a very young man, of about nineteen, perhaps even less—to judge from the youthfulness of his handsome, self-confident, upturned face. He was fairly well dressed, or at any rate his clothes looked well on him; in height he was a little above the average; the black hair that hung in thick locks about his head, and the big, bold, dark eyes were particularly conspicuous in his face. Except that his nose was rather broad and turned up, he was a handsome fellow. He walked in solemnly.

"I believe I have the opportunity of conversing with M. Trusotsky," he pronounced in a measured tone, emphasizing with peculiar relish the word "opportunity"—giving him to understand thereby that he did not consider it either an "honour" or a "pleasure" to converse with M. Trusotsky.

Velchaninov began to grasp the position; something seemed to be dawning on Pavel Pavlovitch too. There was a look of uneasiness in his face; but he stood his ground.

"Not having the honour of your acquaintance," he answered majestically, "I imagine that you cannot have business of any sort with me."

"You had better hear me first and then give your opinion," the young man admonished him self-confidently, and, taking out a tortoiseshell lorgnette hanging on a cord, he examined through it the bottle of champagne standing on the table. When he had calmly completed his scrutiny of the bottle, he folded up the lorgnette and turned to Pavel Pavlovitch again.

"Alexandr Lobov."

"What do you mean by Alexandr Lobov?"

"That's me. Haven't you heard of me?"

"No."

"How should you, though? I've come on important business that chiefly concerns you. Allow me to sit down; I'm tired."

"Sit down," Velchaninov urged him; but the young man succeeded in sitting down before being invited to do so.

In spite of the increasing pain in his chest Velchaninov was interested in this impudent youth. In his pretty, childlike and rosy face, he fancied a remote resemblance to Nadya.

"You sit down too," the lad suggested to Pavel Pavlovitch, motioning him with a careless nod of the head to a seat opposite.

"Don't trouble; I'll stand."

"You'll be tired. You needn't go away, M. Velchaninov, if you like to stay."

"I've nowhere to go; I'm at home."

"As you please. I must confess I should prefer you to be present while I have an explanation with this gentleman. Nadyezhda Fedosyevna gave me rather a flattering account of you."

"Bah! When had she time to do that?"

"Why, just now after you left; I've just come from there, too. I've something to tell you, M. Trusotsky." He turned round to Pavel Pavlovitch, who was standing. "We—that is, Nadyezhda Fedosyevna and I," he went on, letting his words drop one by one as he lolled carelessly in the arm-chair; "we've cared for each other for ever so long, and have given each other our promise. You are in our way now; I've come to suggest that you should clear out. Will it suit you to act on my suggestion?"

Pavel Pavlovitch positively reeled; he turned pale, but a diabolical smile came on to his lips at once.

"No, it won't suit me at all," he rapped out laconically.

"You don't say so!" The young man turned round in the arm-chair and crossed one leg over the other.

"I don't know who it is I'm speaking to," added Pavel Pavlovitch.

"I believe, indeed, that there's no object in continuing our conversation."

Uttering this, he too thought fit to sit down.

"I told you you would be tired," the youth observed casually. "I told you just now that my name is Alexandr Lobov, and that Nadyezhda and I are pledged to one another; consequently you can't say, as you did just now, that you don't know who it is you have to deal with; you can't imagine, either, that I have nothing more to say to you; putting myself aside, it concerns Nadyezhda Fedosyevna, whom you persist in pestering so insolently. And that alone is sufficient reason for an explanation."

All this he let drop, word by word, through his closed lips, with the air of a coxcomb who did not deign to articulate his words; he even drew out his lorgnette again and turned it upon something while he was talking.

"Excuse me, young man!" Pavel Pavlovitch exclaimed irritably; but the young man instantly snubbed him.

"At any other time I should certainly forbid your calling me 'young man,' but now you will admit that my youth is my chief advantage over you, and that you would have been jolly glad, this morning, for instance, when you presented your bracelet, to be a tiny bit younger."

"Ah, you sprat!" murmured Velchaninov.

"In any case, sir," Pavel Pavlovitch corrected himself with dignity, "I do not consider the reasons you have advanced—most unseemly and dubious reasons—sufficient to continue discussing them. I see that this is all a foolish and childish business. To-morrow I'll make inquiries of my highly respected friend, Fedosey Semyonovitch; and now I beg you to retire."

"Do you see the sort of man he is?" the youth cried at once, unable to sustain his previous tone, and turning hotly to Velchaninov. "It's not enough for him that they've put out their tongues at him to-day and kicked him out—he'll go to-morrow to tell tales of us to the old man! Won't you prove by that, you obstinate man, that you want to take the girl by force, that you want to buy her of people in their dotage who in our barbarous state of society retain authority over her? I should have thought it would have been enough for you that she's shown you how she despises you; why, she gave you back your indecent present to-day, your bracelet. What more do you want?"

"No one has returned me a bracelet, and it's utterly out of the question!" Pavel Pavlovitch said, startled.

"Out of the question? Do you mean to say M. Velchaninov has not given it you?"

"Damnation take you!" thought Velchaninov. "Nadyezhda Fedosyevna did commission me," he said, frowning, "to give you this case, Pavel Pavlovitch. I refused to take it, but she begged me . . . here it is . . . I'm annoyed. . . ."

He took out the case and, much embarrassed, laid it before Pavel Pavlovitch, who was struck dumb.

"Why didn't you give it to him before?" said the young gentleman, addressing Velchaninov severely.

"As you see, I hadn't managed to do so yet," the latter replied, frowning.

"That's queer."

"Wha-a-at?"

"You must admit it's queer, anyway. Though I am ready to allow there may be a misunderstanding."

Velchaninov felt a great inclination to get up at once and pull the saucy urchin's ears, but he could not refrain from bursting out laughing in his face; the boy promptly laughed too. It was very different with Pavel Pavlovitch; if Velchaninov could have observed the terrible look he turned upon him when Velchaninov was laughing at Lobov, he would have realized that at that instant the man was passing through a momentous crisis. . . . But though Velchaninov did not see that glance, he felt that he must stand by Pavel Pavlovitch.

"Listen, M. Lobov," he began in a friendly tone; "without entering into discussion of other reasons upon which I don't care to touch, I would only point out to you that, in paying his addresses to Nadyezhda Fedosyevna, Pavel Pavlovitch can in any case boast of certain qualifications: in the first place, the fact that everything about him is known to that estimable family; in the second place, his excellent and highly respectable position; finally, his fortune, and consequently he must naturally be surprised at the sight of a rival like you—a man, perhaps, of great merit, but so exceedingly young that he can hardly take you for a serious suitor . . . and so he is justified in asking you to retire."

"What do you mean by 'exceedingly young'? I was nineteen last month. By law I could have been married long ago. That is all I can say."

But what father could bring himself to give you his daughter now—even if you were to be a millionaire in the future or some benefactor of mankind? At nineteen a man cannot even answer for himself, and you are ready to take the responsibility of another person's future, that is, the future of another child like yourself! Why, do you think it's quite honourable? I have ventured to speak frankly to you because you appealed to me just now as an intermediary between you and Pavel Pavlovitch."

"Ah, to be sure, his name's Pavel Pavlovitch!" observed the boy; "how is it I kept fancying that he was Vassily Petrovitch? Well," he went on, addressing Velchaninov, "you haven't surprised me in the least; I knew you were all like that! It's odd, though, that they talked of you as a man rather new in a way. But that's all nonsense, though; far from there being anything dishonourable on my part, as you so freely expressed it, it's the very opposite, as I hope to make you see: to begin with, we've pledged our word to each other, and, what's more, I've promised her, before two witnesses, that if she ever falls in love with some one else, or simply regrets having married me and wants to separate, I will at once give her a formal declaration of my infidelity— and so will support her petition for divorce. What's more, in case I should later on go back upon my word and refuse to give her that declaration, I will give her as security on our wedding-day an I O U for a hundred thousand roubles, so that if I should be perverse about the declaration she can at once change my I O U and me into the bargain! In that way everything will be secured and I shouldn't be risking anybody's future. That's the first point."

"I bet that fellow—What's-his-name?—Predposylov invented that for you!" cried Velchaninov.

"He, he, he!" chuckled Pavel Pavlovitch viciously.

"What's that gentleman sniggering about? You guessed right, it was Predposylov's idea; and you must admit it was a shrewd one. The absurd law is completely paralyzed by it. Of course, I intend to love her for ever, and she laughs tremendously; at the same time it's ingenious, and you must admit that it's honourable, and that it's not every man who would consent to do it."

"To my thinking, so far from being honourable, it's positively disgusting."

The young man shrugged his shoulders.

"Again you don't surprise me," he observed, after a brief silence. "I have given up being surprised at that sort of thing long ago. Predposylov would tell you flatly that your lack of comprehension of the most natural things is due to the corruption of your most ordinary feelings and ideas by a long life spent idly and absurdly. But possibly we don't understand one another; they spoke well of you anyway . . . you're fifty, I suppose, aren't you?"

"Kindly keep to the point."

"Excuse my indiscretion and don't be annoyed; I didn't mean anything. I will continue: I'm by no means a future millionaire, as you expressed it (and what an idea!); I have nothing but what I stand up in, but I have complete confidence in my future. I shan't be a hero or a benefactor of mankind either, but I shall keep myself and my wife. Of course, I've nothing now; I was brought up in their house, you see, from childhood. . . ."

"How was that?"

"Well, you see, I'm the son of a distant relation of Zahlebinin's wife, and when all my people died and left me at eight years old, the old man took me in and afterwards sent me to the high school. He's really a good-natured man, if you care to know. . . ."

"I know that."

"Yes; a bit antiquated in his ideas, but kind-hearted. It's a long time now, of course, since I was under his guardianship; I want to earn my own living, and to owe no one anything."

"How long have you been independent?" Velchaninov inquired.

"Why, four months."

"Oh, well, one can understand it then: you've been friends from childhood! Well, have you a situation, then?"

"Yes, a private situation, in a notary's office, for twenty-five roubles a month. Of course, only for the time, but when I made my offer I hadn't even that. I was serving on the railway then for ten roubles a month, but only for the time."

"Do you mean to say you've made an offer of marriage?"

"Yes, a formal offer, and ever so long ago—over three weeks."

"Well, and what happened?"

"The old man laughed awfully at first, and then was awfully angry, and locked her up upstairs. But Nadya held out heroically. But that was all because he was a bit crusty with me before, for throwing up the berth in his department which he had got me into four months ago, before I went to the railway. He's a capital old chap, I tell you again, simple and jolly at home, but you can't fancy what he's like as soon as he's in his office! He's like a Jove enthroned! I naturally let him know that I was not attracted by his manners there, but the chief trouble was through the head clerk's assistant: that gentleman took it into his head that I had been 'rude' to him, and all that I said to him was that he was undeveloped. I threw them all up, and now I'm at a notary's."

"And did you get much in the department?"

"Oh, I was not on the regular staff! The old man used to give me an allowance too; I tell you he's a good sort, but we shan't give in, all the same. Of course, twenty-five roubles is not enough to support a wife, but I hope soon to have a share in the management of Count Zavileysky's neglected estates, and then to rise to three thousand straight off, or else I shall become a lawyer. People are always going to law nowadays. . . . Bah! What a clap of thunder! There'll be a storm; it's a good thing I managed to get here before it; I came on foot, I ran almost all the way."

"But, excuse me, if so, when did you manage to talk things over with Nadyezhda Fedosyevna, especially if they refuse you admittance?"

"Why, one can talk over the fence! Did you notice that red-haired girl?" he laughed. "She's very active on our side, and Marie Nikititchna too; ah, she's a serpent, that Marie Nikititchna! . . . Why do you wince? Are you afraid of the thunder?"

"No, I'm unwell, very unwell. . . ."

Velchaninov, in positive agony from the pain in his chest, got up and tried to walk about the room.

"Oh, then, of course, I'm in your way. . . . Don't be uneasy, I'm just going!"

And the youth jumped up from his seat.

"You're not in the way; it's no matter," said Velchaninov courteously.

"How can it be no matter? 'When Kobylnikov had a stomach-ache' . . . do you remember in Shtchedrin? Are you fond of Shtchedrin?"

"Yes."

"So am I. Well, Vassily . . . oh, hang it, Pavel Pavlovitch, let's finish!" He turned, almost laughing, to Pavel Pavlovitch. "I will once more for your comprehension formulate the question: do you consent to make a formal withdrawal of all pretensions in regard to Nadyezhda Fedosyevna to the old people to-morrow, in my presence?"

"I certainly do not." Pavel Pavlovitch, too, got up from his seat with an impatient and exasperated air. "And I beg you once more to spare me . . . for all this is childish and silly."

"You had better look out." The youth held up a warning finger with a supercilious smile. "Don't make a mistake in your calculations! Do you know what such a mistake leads to? I warn you that in nine months' time, when you have had all your expense and trouble, and you come back here, you'll be forced to give up Nadyezhda Fedosyevna, or if you don't give her up it will be the worse for you; that's what will be the end of it! I must warn you that you're like the dog in the manger—excuse me, it's only a comparison—getting nothing yourself and preventing others. From motives of humanity I tell you again: reflect upon it, force yourself for once in your life to reflect rationally."

"I beg you to spare me your sermonizing!" cried Pavel Pavlovitch furiously; "and as for your nasty insinuations, I shall take measures to-morrow, severe measures!"

"Nasty insinuations? What do you mean by that? You're nasty yourself, if that's what you've got in your head. However, I agree to

wait till to-morrow, but if . . . Ah, thunder again! Good-bye; very glad
to make your acquaintance"—he nodded to Velchaninov and ran off,
apparently in haste to get back before the storm and not to get caught
in the rain.

15. THE ACCOUNT IS SETTLED

"You see? You see?" Pavel Pavlovitch skipped up to Velchaninov as
soon as the youth had departed.

"Yes; you've no luck!" said Velchaninov carelessly.

He would not have said those words had he not been tortured and
exasperated by the pain in his chest, which was growing more and
more acute.

"It was because you felt for me, you didn't give me back the
bracelet, wasn't it?"

"I hadn't time. . . ."

"You felt for me from your heart, like a true friend?"

"Oh yes, I felt for you," said Velchaninov, in exasperation.

He told him briefly, however, how the bracelet had been returned
to him, and how Nadyezhda Fedosyevna had almost forced him to assist in returning it. . . .

"You understand that nothing else would have induced me to take
it; I've had unpleasantness enough apart from that!"

"You were fascinated and took it?" sniggered Pavel Pavlovitch.

"That's stupid on your part; however, I must excuse you. You saw
for yourself just now that I'm not the leading person, that there are
others in this affair."

"At the same time you were fascinated."

Pavel Pavlovitch sat down and filled up his glass.

"Do you imagine I'd give way to that wretched boy? I'll make
mincemeat of him, so there! I'll go over to-morrow and polish him
off. We'll smoke out that spirit from the nursery."

He emptied his glass almost at a gulp and filled it again; he began,
in fact, to behave in an unusually free and easy way.

"Ah, Nadenka and Sashenka, the sweet little darlings, he-he-he!"

He was beside himself with anger. There came another louder clap
of thunder, followed by a blinding flash of lightning, and the rain
began streaming in bucketfuls. Pavel Pavlovitch got up and closed the
open window.

"He asked you whether you were afraid of the thunder, he-he.
Velchaninov afraid of thunder! Kobylnikov—what was it—

Kobylnikov . . . and what about being fifty too—eh? Do you remember?" Pavel Pavlovitch sneered diabolically.

"You've established yourself here, it seems!" observed Velchaninov, hardly able to articulate the words for the pain in his chest. "I'll lie down, you can do what you like."

"Why, you couldn't turn a dog out in weather like this!" Pavel Pavlovitch retorted in an aggrieved tone, seeming almost pleased, however, at having an excuse for feeling aggrieved.

"All right, sit down, drink . . . stay the night, if you like!" muttered Velchaninov. He stretched himself on the sofa and uttered a faint groan.

"Stay the night? And you won't be afraid?"

"What of?" said Velchaninov, suddenly raising his head.

"Oh, nothing. Last time you were so frightened, or was it my fancy?"

"You're stupid!" Velchaninov could not help saying. He turned his head to the wall angrily.

"All right," responded Pavel Pavlovitch.

The sick man fell asleep suddenly, a minute after lying down. The unnatural strain upon him that day in the shattered state of his health had brought on a sudden crisis, and he was as weak as a child. But the pain asserted itself again and got the upper hand of sleep and weariness; an hour later he woke up and painfully got up from the sofa. The storm had subsided; the room was full of tobacco smoke, on the table stood an empty bottle, and Pavel Pavlovitch was asleep on another sofa. He was lying on his back, with his head on the sofa cushion, fully dressed and with his boots on. His lorgnette had slipped out of his pocket and was hanging down almost to the floor. His hat was lying on the ground beside it. Velchaninov looked at him morosely and did not attempt to wake him. Writhing with pain and pacing about the room, for he could no longer bear to lie down, he moaned and brooded over his agonies.

He was afraid of that pain in his chest, and not without reason. He had been liable to these attacks for a very long time, but they had only occurred at intervals of a year or two. He knew that they came from the liver. At first a dull, not acute, but irritating feeling of oppression was, as it were, concentrated at some point in the chest, under the shoulder-blade or higher up. Continually increasing, sometimes for ten hours at a stretch, the pain at last would reach such a pitch, the oppression would become so insupportable, that the sufferer began to have visions of dying. On his last attack, a year before, he was, when the pain ceased after ten hours of suffering, so weak that he could scarcely move his hands as he lay in bed, and the doctor had allowed him to take nothing for the whole day but a few teaspoonfuls of weak tea and of bread soaked in broth, like a tiny baby. The attacks were brought on by different things, but never occurred except when his nerves were out of order. It was strange, too, how the attack passed off; sometimes it was possible to arrest it at the very beginning, during the first half-hour, by simple compresses, and it would pass away completely at once; sometimes, as on his last attack, nothing was of any use, and the pain only subsided after numerous and continually recurring paroxysms of vomiting. The doctor confessed afterwards that he believed it to be a case of poisoning. It was a long time to wait till morning, and he didn't want to send for the doctor at night; besides, he didn't like doctors. At last he could not control himself and began moaning aloud. His groans waked Pavel Pavlovitch; he sat up on the sofa, and for some time listened with alarm and bewilderment, watching Velchaninov, who was almost running backwards and forwards through the two rooms. The bottle of champagne had had a great effect upon him, evidently more than usual, and it was some time before he could collect himself. At last he grasped the position and rushed to Velchaninov, who mumbled something in reply to him.

"It's the liver, I know it!" cried Pavel Pavlovitch, becoming extremely animated all at once. "Pyotr Kuzmitch Polosuhin used to suffer just the same from liver. You ought to have compresses. Pyotr Kuzmitch always had compresses. . . . One may die of it! Shall I run for Mavra?"

"No need, no need!" Velchaninov waved him off irritably. "I want nothing."

But Pavel Pavlovitch, goodness knows why, seemed beside himself, as though it were a question of saving his own son. Without heeding Velchaninov's protests, he insisted on the necessity of compresses and also of two or three cups of weak tea to be drunk on the spot, "and not simply hot, but boiling!" He ran to Mavra, without waiting for permission, with her laid a fire in the kitchen, which always stood empty, and blew up the samovar; at the same time he succeeded in getting the sick man to bed, took off his clothes, wrapped him up in a quilt, and within twenty minutes had prepared tea and compresses.

"This is a hot plate, scalding hot!" he said, almost ecstatically, applying the heated plate, wrapped up in a napkin, on Velchaninov's aching chest. "There are no other compresses, and plates, I swear on my honour, will be even better: they were laid on Pyotr Kuzmitch, I saw it with my own eyes, and did it with my own hands. One may die of it, you know. Drink your tea, swallow it; never mind about scalding yourself; life is too precious . . . for one to be squeamish."

He quite flustered Mavra, who was half asleep; the plates were changed every three or four minutes. After the third plate and the second cup of tea, swallowed at a gulp, Velchaninov felt a sudden relief.

"If once they've shifted the pain, thank God, it's a good sign!" cried Pavel Pavlovitch, and he ran joyfully to fetch a fresh plate and a fresh cup of tea.

"If only we can ease the pain. If only we can keep it under!" he kept repeating.

Half an hour later the pain was much less, but the sick man was so exhausted that in spite of Pavel Pavlovitch's entreaties he refused to "put up with just one more nice little plate." He was so weak that everything was dark before his eyes.

"Sleep, sleep," he repeated in a faint voice.

"To be sure," Pavel Pavlovitch assented.

"You'll stay the night. . . . What time is it?"

"It's nearly two o'clock, it's a quarter to."

"You'll stay the night."

"I will, I will."

A minute later the sick man called Pavel Pavlovitch again.

"You, you," he muttered, when the latter had run up and was bending over him; "you are better than I am! I understand it all, all. . . . Thank you."

"Sleep, sleep," whispered Pavel Pavlovitch, and he hastened on tiptoe to his sofa.

As he fell asleep the invalid heard Pavel Pavlovitch noiselessly making up a bed for himself and taking off his clothes. Finally, putting out the candle, and almost holding his breath for fear of waking the patient, he stretched himself on his sofa.

There is no doubt that Velchaninov did sleep and that he fell asleep very soon after the candle was put out; he remembered this clearly afterwards. But all the time he was asleep, up to the very moment that he woke up, he dreamed that he was not asleep, and that in spite of his exhaustion he could not get to sleep. At last he began to dream that he was in a sort of waking delirium, and that he could not drive away the phantoms that crowded about him, although he was fully conscious that it was only delirium and not reality. The phantoms were all familiar figures; his room seemed to be full of people; and the door into the passage stood open; people were coming in in crowds and thronging the stairs. At the table, which was set in the middle of the room, there was sitting one man—exactly as in the similar dream he had had a month before. Just as in that dream, this man sat with his elbows on the table and would not speak; but this time he was wearing a round hat with crape on it. "What! could it have been Pavel Pavlovitch that time too?" Velchaninov thought, but, glancing at the face of the silent man, he convinced himself that it was some one quite different. "Why has he got crape on?" Velchaninov wondered. The noise, the talking and the shouting of the people crowding round the table, was awful. These people seemed to be even more intensely exasperated against Velchaninov than in the previous dream; they shook their fists at him, and shouted something to him with all their might, but what it was exactly he could not make out. "But it's delirium, of course, I know it's delirium!" he thought; "I know I couldn't get to sleep and that I've got up now, because it made me too wretched to go on lying down. . . ." But the shouts, the people, their gestures were so lifelike, so real, that sometimes he was seized by doubt: 'Can this be really delirium? Good heavens! What do these people want of me? But . . . if it were not an hallucination, would it be possible that such a clamour should not have waked Pavel Pavlovitch all this time? There he is asleep on the sofa!" At last something suddenly happened again, just as in that other dream; all of them made a rush for the stairs and they were closely packed in the doorway, for there was another crowd forcing its way into the room. These people were bringing something in with them, something big and heavy; he could hear how heavily the steps of those carrying it sounded on the stairs and how hurriedly their panting voices called to one another. All the people in the room shouted: "They're bringing it, they're bringing it"—all eyes were flashing and fixed on Velchaninov; all of them pointed towards the stairs, menacing and triumphant. Feeling no further doubt that it was reality and not hallucination, he stood on tiptoe so as to peep over the people's heads and find out as soon as possible what they were bringing up the stairs. His heart was beating, beating, beating, and suddenly, exactly as in that first dream, he heard three violent rings at the bell. And again it was so distinct, so real, so unmistakable a ring at the bell, that it could not be only a dream. . . .

But he did not rush to the door as he had done on awaking then. What idea guided his first movement and whether he had any idea at the moment it is impossible to say, but some one seemed to prompt him what he must do: he leapt out of bed and, with his hands stretched out before him as though to defend himself and ward off an attack, rushed straight towards the place where Pavel Pavlovitch was asleep. His hands instantly came into contact with other hands, stretched out above him, and he clutched them tight; so, some one already stood bending over him. The curtains were drawn, but it was not quite dark, for a faint light came from the other room where there were no such curtains. Suddenly, with an acute pain, something cut the palm and fingers of his left hand, and he instantly realized that he had clutched the blade of a knife or razor and was grasping it tight in his hand. . . . And at the same moment something fell heavily on the floor with a thud.

Velchaninov was perhaps three times as strong as Pavel Pavlovitch, yet the struggle between them lasted a long while, fully three minutes. He soon got him down on the floor and bent his arms back behind him, but for some reason he felt he must tie his hands behind him. Holding the murderer with his wounded left hand, he began with his right fumbling for the cord of the window curtain and for a long time could not find it, but at last got hold of it and tore it from the window. He wondered himself afterwards at the immense effort required to do this. During those three minutes neither of them uttered a word; nothing was audible but their heavy breathing and the muffled sounds of their struggling. Having at last twisted Pavel Pavlovitch's arms behind him and tied them together, Velchaninov left him on the floor, got up, drew the curtain from the window and pulled up the blind. It was already light in the deserted street. Opening the window, he stood for some moments drawing in deep breaths of fresh air. It was a little past four. Shutting the window, he went hurriedly to the cupboard, took out a clean towel and bound it tightly round his left hand to stop the bleeding. At his feet an open razor was lying on the carpet; he picked it up, shut it, put it in the razor-case, which had been left forgotten since the morning on the little table beside Pavel Pavlovitch's sofa, and locked it up in his bureau. And, only when he had done all that, he went up to Pavel Pavlovitch and began to examine him.

Meantime, the latter had with an effort got up from the floor, and seated himself in an arm-chair. He had nothing on but his shirt, not even his boots. The back and the sleeves of his shirt were soaked with blood; but the blood was not his own, it came from Velchaninov's wounded hand. Of course it was Pavel Pavlovitch, but any one meeting him by chance might almost have failed to recognize him at the minute, so changed was the whole appearance. He was sitting awkwardly upright in the arm-chair, owing to his hands being tied behind his back, his face looked distorted, exhausted and greenish, and he quivered all over from time to time. He looked at Velchaninov fixedly, but with lustreless, unseeing eyes. All at once he smiled vacantly, and, nodding towards a bottle of water that stood on the table, he said in a meek half-whisper—

"Water, I should like some water."

Velchaninov filled a glass and began holding it for him to drink. Pavel Pavlovitch bent down greedily to the water; after three gulps he raised his head and looked intently into the face of Velchaninov, who was standing beside him with the glass in his hand, but without utter-

ing a word he fell to drinking again. When he had finished he sighed
deeply. Velchaninov took his pillow, seized his outer garments and
went into the other room, locking Pavel Pavlovitch into the first
room.

The pain had passed off completely, but he was conscious of extreme weakness again after the momentary effort in which he had
displayed an unaccountable strength. He tried to reflect upon
what had happened, but his thoughts were hardly coherent, the
shock had been too great. Sometimes there was a dimness before
his eyes lasting for ten minutes or so, then he would start, wake
up, recollect everything, remember his smarting hand bound up in
a blood-stained towel, and would fall to thinking greedily, feverishly. He came to one distinct conclusion—that is, that Pavel
Pavlovitch certainly had meant to cut his throat, but that perhaps
only a quarter of an hour before had not known that he would do
it. The razor-case had perhaps merely caught his eye the evening
before, and, without arousing any thought of it at the time, had remained in his memory. (The razors were always locked up in the
bureau, and only the morning before, Velchaninov had taken
them out to shave round his moustache and whiskers, as he sometimes did.)

"If he had long been intending to murder me he would have got a
knife or pistol ready; he would not have reckoned on my razor, which
he had never seen till yesterday evening," was one reflection he made
among others.

It struck six o'clock at last; Velchaninov roused himself, dressed,
and went in to Pavel Pavlovitch. Opening the door, he could not understand why he had locked Pavel Pavlovitch in, instead of turning
him out of the house. To his surprise, the criminal was fully dressed;
most likely he had found some way of untying his hands. He was sitting in the arm-chair, but got up at once when Velchaninov went in.
His hat was already in his hand. His uneasy eyes seemed in haste to
say—

"Don't begin talking; it's no use beginning; there's no need to talk."

"Go," said Velchaninov. "Take your bracelet," he added, calling
after him.

Pavel Pavlovitch turned back from the door, took the case with the
bracelet from the table, put it in his pocket and went out on the stairs.
Velchaninov stood at the door to lock it behind him. Their eyes met
for the last time; Pavel Pavlovitch stopped suddenly, for five seconds
the two looked into each other's eyes—as though hesitating; finally
Velchaninov waved his hand faintly.

"Well, go!" he said in a low voice, and locked the door.

16. ANALYSIS

A feeling of immense, extraordinary relief took possession of him; something was over, was settled; an awful weight of depression had vanished and was dissipated for ever. So it seemed to him. It had lasted for five weeks. He raised his hand, looked at the towel soaked with blood and muttered to himself: "Yes, now everything is absolutely at an end!" And all that morning, for the first time in three weeks, he scarcely thought of Liza—as though that blood from his cut fingers could "settle his account" even with that misery.

He recognized clearly that he had escaped a terrible danger. "These people," he thought, "just these people who don't know a minute beforehand whether they'll murder a man or not—as soon as they take a knife in their trembling hands and feel the hot spurt of blood on their fingers don't stick at cutting your throat, but cut off your head, 'clean off,' as convicts express it. That is so."

He could not remain at home and went out into the street, feeling convinced that he must do something, or something would happen to him at once; he walked about the streets and waited. He had an intense longing to meet some one, to talk to some one, even to a stranger, and it was only that which led him at last to think of a doctor and of the necessity of binding up his hand properly. The doctor, an old acquaintance of his, examined the wound, and inquired with interest how it could have happened. Velchaninov laughed and was on the point of telling him all about it, but restrained himself. The doctor was obliged to feel his pulse and, hearing of his attack the night before, persuaded him to take some soothing medicine he had at hand. He was reassuring about the cuts: "They could have no particularly disagreeable results." Velchaninov laughed and began to assure him that they had already had the most agreeable results. An almost irresistible desire to tell the whole story came over him twice again during that day, on one occasion to a total stranger with whom he entered into conversation at a tea-shop. He had never been able to endure entering into conversation with strangers in public places before.

He went into a shop to buy a newspaper; he went to his tailor's and ordered a suit. The idea of visiting the Pogoryeltsevs was still distasteful to him, and he did not think of them, and indeed he could not have gone to their villa: he kept expecting something here in the town. He dined with enjoyment, he talked to the waiter and to his fellow-diners, and drank half a bottle of wine. The possibility of the return of his illness of the day before did not occur to him; he was convinced that the illness had passed off completely at the moment when, after falling asleep so exhausted, he had, an hour and a half later, sprung out of bed and thrown his assailant on the floor with such strength. Towards evening he began to feel giddy, and at moments was overcome by something like the delirium he had had in his sleep. It was dusk when he returned home, and he was almost afraid of his room when he went into it. It seemed dreadful and uncanny in his flat. He walked up and down it several times, and even went into his kitchen, where he had scarcely ever been before. "Here they were heating plates yesterday," he thought. He locked the door securely and lighted the candles earlier than usual. As he locked the door he remembered, half an hour before, passing the porter's lodge, he had called Mavra and asked her whether Pavel Pavlovitch had come in his absence, as though he could possibly have come.

After locking himself in carefully, he opened the bureau, took out the razor-case and opened the razor to look at it again. On the white bone handle there were still faint traces of blood. He put the razor back in the case and locked it up in the bureau again. He felt sleepy; he felt that he must go to bed at once—or "he would not be fit for to-morrow." He pictured the next day for some reason as a momentous and "decisive" day.

But the same thoughts that had haunted him all day in the street kept incessantly and persistently crowding and jostling in his sick brain, and he kept thinking, thinking, thinking, and for a long time could not get to sleep. . . ."

"If it is settled that he tried to murder me *accidentally,*" he went on pondering, "had the idea ever entered his head before, if only as a dream in a vindictive moment?"

He decided that question strangely—that "Pavel Pavlovitch did want to kill him, but the thought of the murder had never entered his head." In short: "Pavel Pavlovitch wanted to kill him, but didn't know he wanted to kill him. It's senseless, but that's the truth," thought Velchaninov. "It was not to get a post and it was not on Bagautov's account he came here, though he did try to get a post here, and did run to see Bagautov and was furious when he died; he thought no more of him than a chip. He came here on my account and he came here with Liza . . .

"And did I expect that he . . . would murder me?" He decided that he did, that he had expected it from the moment when he saw him in the carriage following Bagautov's funeral. "I began, as it were, to expect something . . . but, of course, not that; but, of course, not that he would murder me! . . .

"And can it be that all that was true?" he exclaimed again, suddenly raising his head from the pillow and opening his eyes. "All that that

. . . madman told me yesterday about his love for me, when his chin quivered and he thumped himself on the breast with his fist?

"It was the absolute truth," he decided, still pondering and analyzing, "that Quasimodo from T—— was quite sufficiently stupid and noble to fall in love with the lover of his wife, about whom he noticed nothing suspicious in twenty years! He had been thinking of me with respect, cherishing my memory and brooding over my utterances for nine years. Good heavens! and I had no notion of it! He could not have been lying yesterday! But did he love me yesterday when he declared his feeling and said 'Let us settle our account'? Yes, it was from hatred that he loved me; that's the strongest of all loves . . .

"Of course it may have happened, of course it must have happened that I made a tremendous impression on him at T——. Tremendous and 'gratifying' is just what it was, and it's just with a Schiller like that, in the outer form of a Quasimodo, that such a thing could happen! He magnified me a hundredfold because I impressed him too much in his philosophic solitude. . . . It would be interesting to know by what I impressed him. Perhaps by my clean gloves and my knowing how to put them on. Quasimodos are fond of all that is aesthetic. Ough! aren't they fond of it! A glove is often quite enough for a noble heart, and especially one of these 'eternal husbands.' The rest they supply themselves a thousand times, and are ready to fight for you, to satisfy your slightest wish. What an opinion he had of my powers of fascination! Perhaps it was just my powers of fascination that made the most impression on him. And his cry then, 'If that one, too . . . whom can one trust!' After that cry one may well become a wild beast! . . .

"H'm! He comes here 'to embrace me and to weep,' as he expressed it in the most abject way—that is, he came here to murder me and thought he came 'to embrace me and to weep.' . . . He brought Liza too. But, who knows? if I had wept with him, perhaps, really, he would have forgiven me, for he had a terrible longing to forgive me! . . . At the first shock all that was changed into drunken antics and caricature, and into loathsome, womanish whining over his wrongs. (Those horns! those horns he made on his forehead!) He came drunk on purpose to speak out, though he was playing the fool; if he had not been drunk, even he could not have done it. . . . And how he liked playing the fool, didn't he like it! Ough! wasn't he pleased, too, when he made me kiss him! Only he didn't know then whether he would end by embracing me or murdering me. Of course, it's turned out that the best thing was to do both. A most natural solution! Yes indeed, nature dislikes monstrosities and destroys them with natural solutions. The most monstrous monster is the monster with noble feelings; I know that by personal experience, Pavel Pavlovitch! Nature is not a tender mother, but a stepmother to the monster. Nature gives birth to the deformed, but instead of pitying him she punishes him, and with good reason. Even decent people have to pay for embraces and tears of forgiveness nowadays, to say nothing of men like you and me, Pavel Pavlovitch!

"Yes, he was stupid enough to take me to see his future bride. Good heavens! His future bride! Only a Quasimodo like that could have conceived the notion of 'rising again to a new life' by means of the innocence of Mademoiselle Zahlebinin! But it was not your fault, Pavel Pavlovitch, it was not your fault: you're a monster, so everything about you is bound to be monstrous, your dreams and your hopes. But, though he was a monster, he had doubts of his dream, and that was why he needed the high sanction of Velchaninov whom he so revered. He wanted Velchaninov to approve, he wanted him to reassure him that the dream was not a dream, but something real. He took me there from a devout respect for me and faith in the nobility of my feelings, believing, perhaps, that there, under a bush, we should embrace and shed tears near all that youthful innocence. Yes! That 'eternal husband' was obliged, sooner or later, to punish himself for everything, and to punish himself he snatched up the razor—by accident, it is true, still he did snatch it up! 'And yet he stuck him with a knife, and yet he ended by stabbing him in the presence of the Governor.' And, by the way, had he any idea of that sort in his mind when he told me that anecdote about the best man? And was there really anything that night when he got out of bed and stood in the middle of the room? H'm! . . . No, he stood there then *as a joke*. He got up for other reasons, and when he saw that I was frightened of him he did not answer me for ten minutes because he was very much pleased that I was frightened of him. . . . It was at that moment, perhaps, when he stood there in the dark, that some idea of this sort first dawned upon him. . . .

"Yet if I had not forgotten that razor on the table yesterday—maybe nothing would have happened. Is that so? Is that so? To be sure he had been avoiding me before—why, he had not been to see me for a fortnight; he had been hiding from me to *spare* me! Of course, he picked out Bagautov first, not me! Why, he rushed to heat plates for me in the night, thinking to create a diversion—from the knife to pity and tenderness! . . . He wanted to save himself and me, too—with his hot plates! . . ."

And for a long time the sick brain of this "man of the world" went on working in this way, going round and round in a circle, till he grew calmer. He woke up next morning with the same headache, but with a quite *new* and quite unexpected terror in his heart.

This new terror came from the positive conviction, which suddenly grew strong with him, that he, Velchaninov (a man of the world), would end it all that day by going of his own free will to Pavel Pavlovitch. Why? What for? He had no idea and, with repugnance, refused to know; all that he knew was that, for some reason, he would go to him.

This madness, however—he could give it no other name—did, as it developed, take a rational form and fasten upon a fairly legitimate pretext: he had even, the day before, been haunted by the idea that Pavel Pavlovitch would go back to his lodging and hang himself, like the clerk about whom Marya Sysoevna had told him. This notion of the day before had passed by degrees into an unreasoning but persistent conviction. "Why should the fool hang himself?" he kept protesting to himself every half-minute. He remembered Liza's words . . . "Yet in his place, perhaps, I should hang myself!" . . . he reflected once.

It ended by his turning towards Pavel Pavlovitch instead of going to dinner. "I shall simply inquire of Marya Sysoevna," he decided. But before he had come out into the street he stopped short in the gateway. "Can it be, can it be?" he cried, turning crimson with shame. "Can it be that I'm crawling there, to 'embrace and shed tears'? That senseless abjectness was all that was needed to complete the ignominy!"

But from that "senseless abjectness" he was saved by the providence that watches over all decent and well-bred people. He had no sooner stepped into the street when he stumbled upon Alexandr Lobov. The young man was in breathless haste and excitement.

"I was coming to see you! What do you think of our friend Pavel Pavlovitch, now?"

"He's hanged himself!" Velchaninov muttered wildly.

"Who's hanged himself? What for?" cried Lobov, with wide-open eyes.

"Never mind . . . I didn't mean anything; go on."

"Tfoo! damn it all! what funny ideas you have, though. He's not hanged himself at all (why should he hang himself?). On the contrary—he's gone away. I've only just put him into the train and seen him off. Tfoo! how he drinks, I tell you! We drank three bottles, Predposylov with us—but how he drinks, how he drinks! He was singing songs in the train. He remembered you, blew kisses, sent you his greetings. But he is a scoundrel, don't you think so?"

The young man certainly was a little tipsy; his flushed face, his shining eyes and faltering tongue betrayed it unmistakably.

Velchaninov laughed loudly.

"So in the end they finished up with Brüderschaft! Ha-ha! They embraced and shed tears! Ah, you Schilleresque poets!"

"Don't call me names, please. Do you know he's given it all up over *there?* He was there yesterday, and he's been there to-day. He sneaked horribly. They locked Nadya up—she's sitting in a room upstairs. There were tears and lamentations, but we stood firm! But how he does drink, I say, doesn't he drink! And, I say, isn't he *mauvais ton,*★ at least not *mauvais ton* exactly, what shall I call it? . . . He kept talking of you, but there's no comparison between you! You're a gentleman anyway, and really did move in decent society at one time and have only been forced to come down now through poverty or something. . . . Goodness knows what, I couldn't quite understand him."

"Ah, so he spoke to you of me in those terms?"

"He did, he did; don't be angry. To be a good citizen is better than being in aristocratic society. I say that because in Russia nowadays one doesn't know whom to respect. You'll agree that it's a serious malady of the age, when people don't know whom to respect, isn't it?"

"It is, it is; what did he say?"

"He? Who? Ah, to be sure! Why did he keep saying 'Velchaninov fifty, but a rake,' why *but* a rake and not *and* a rake; he laughed and repeated it a thousand times over. He got into the train, sang a song and burst out crying—it was simply revolting, pitiful, in fact—from drunkenness. Oh! I don't like fools! He fell to throwing money to the beggars for the peace of the soul of Lizaveta—his wife, is that?"

"His daughter."

"What's the matter with your hand?"

"I cut it."

"Never mind, it will get better. Damn him, you know, it's a good thing he's gone, but I bet anything that he'll get married directly he arrives—he will—won't he?"

"Why, but you want to get married, too, don't you?"

"Me? That's a different matter. What a man you are, really! If you are fifty, he must be sixty: you must look at it logically, my dear sir! And do you know I used, long ago, to be a pure Slavophil by conviction, but now we look for dawn from the West. . . . But, good-bye; I'm glad I met you without going in; I won't come in, don't ask me, I've no time to spare! . . ."

And he was just running off.

"Oh, by the way," he cried, turning back; "why, he sent me to you with a letter! Here is the letter. Why didn't you come to see him off?"

★ Poorly mannered.

Velchaninov returned home and opened the envelope addressed to him.

There was not one line from Pavel Pavlovitch in it, but there was a different letter. Velchaninov recognized the handwriting. It was an old letter, written on paper yellow with age, with ink that had changed colour. It had been written to him ten years before, two months after he had left T—— and returned to Petersburg. But the letter had never reached him; he had received a different one instead of it; this was clear from the contents of this old yellow letter. In this letter Natalya Vassilyevna took leave of him for ever, and confessed that she loved some one else, just as in the letter he had actually received; but she also did not conceal from him that she was going to have a child. On the contrary, to comfort him, she held out hopes that she might find a possibility of handing over the future child to him, declared henceforth that they had other duties—in short, there was little logic, but the object was clear: that he should no longer trouble her with his love. She even sanctioned his coming to T—— in a year's time to have a look at the child. God knows why she changed her mind and sent the other letter instead.

Velchaninov was pale as he read it, but he pictured to himself Pavel Pavlovitch finding that letter and reading it for the first time, before the opened ebony box inlaid with mother-of-pearl which was an heirloom in the family.

"He too, must have turned pale as a corpse," he thought, catching a glimpse of his own face in the looking-glass. "He must have read it and closed his eyes, and opened them again hoping that the letter would have changed into plain white paper. . . . Most likely he had done that a second time and a third! . . ."

17. THE ETERNAL HUSBAND

Almost exactly two years had passed since the incidents we have described. We meet Velchaninov again on a beautiful summer day, in the train on one of our newly opened railways. He was going to Odessa for his own pleasure, to see one of his friends, and also with a view to something else of an agreeable nature. He hoped through that friend to arrange a meeting with an extremely interesting woman whose acquaintance he had long been eager to make. Without going into details we will confine ourselves to observing that he had become entirely transformed, or rather reformed, during those two years. Of his old hypochondria scarcely a trace remained. Of the various "reminis-

cences" and anxiety—the result of illness which had beset him two
years before in Petersburg at the time of his unsuccessful lawsuit—
nothing remained but a certain secret shame at the consciousness of
his faint-heartedness. What partly made up for it was the conviction
that it would never happen again, and that no one would ever know
of it. It was true that at that time he had given up all society, had even
begun to be slovenly in his dress, had crept away out of sight of every
one—and that, of course, must have been noticed by all. But he so
readily acknowledged his transgressions, and at the same time with
such a self-confident air of new life and vigour, that "every one" immediately forgave his momentary falling away; in fact, those whom he
had given up greeting were the first to recognize him and hold out
their hands, and without any tiresome questions—just as though he
had been absent on his own personal affairs, which were no business
of theirs, and had only just come back from a distance. The cause of
all these salutary changes for the better was, of course, the winning of
his lawsuit. Velchaninov gained in all sixty thousand roubles—no
great sum, of course, but of extreme importance to him; to begin
with, he felt himself on firm ground again, and so he felt satisfied at
heart; he knew for certain now that he would not, "like a fool,"
squander this money, as he had squandered his first two fortunes, and
that he had enough for his whole life. "However the social edifice
may totter, whatever trumpet call they're sounding," he thought
sometimes, as he watched and heard all the marvellous and incredible
things that were being done around him and all over Russia; "whatever shape people and ideas may take, I shall always have just such a
delicate, dainty dinner as I am sitting down to now, and so I'm ready
to face anything." This voluptuous, comfortable thought by degrees
gained complete possession of him and produced a transformation in
his physical, to say nothing of his moral, nature. He looked quite a different man from the "sluggard" whom we have described two years
before and to whom such unseemly incidents had befallen—he
looked cheerful, serene and dignified. Even the ill-humoured wrinkles
that had begun to appear under his eyes and on his forehead had almost been smoothed away; the very tint of his face had changed, his
skin was whiter and ruddier.

At the moment he was sitting comfortably in a first-class carriage
and a charming idea was suggesting itself to his mind. The next station was a junction and there was a new branch line going off to the
right. He asked himself, "How would it be to give up the direct way
for the moment and turn off to the right?" There, only two stations
away, he could visit another lady of his acquaintance who had only
just returned from abroad, and was now living in a provincial isola-

tion, very tedious for her, but favourable for him; and so it would be possible to spend his time no less agreeably than at Odessa, especially as he would not miss his visit there either. But he was still hesitating and could not quite make up his mind; he was waiting for something to decide him. Meanwhile, the station was approaching and that something was not far off.

At this station the train stopped forty minutes, and the passengers had the chance of having dinner. At the entrance to the dining-room for the passengers of the first and second class there was, as there usually is, a crowd of impatient and hurried people, and as is also usual, perhaps, a scandalous scene took place. A lady from a second-class carriage, who was remarkably pretty but somewhat too gorgeously dressed for travelling, was dragging after her an Uhlan, a very young and handsome officer, who was trying to tear himself out of her hands. The youthful officer was extremely drunk, and the lady, to all appearance some elder relative, would not let him go, probably apprehending that he would make a dash for the refreshment bar. Meanwhile, in the crush, the Uhlan was jostled by a young merchant who was also disgracefully intoxicated. He had been hanging about the station for the last two days, drinking and scattering his money among the companions who surrounded him, without succeeding in getting into the train to continue his journey. A scuffle followed; the officer shouted; the merchant swore; the lady was in despair, and, trying to draw the Uhlan away from the conflict, kept exclaiming in an imploring voice, "Mitenka! Mitenka!" This seemed to strike the young merchant as too scandalous; every one laughed, indeed, but the merchant was more offended than ever at the outrage, as he conceived it, on propriety.

"Oh, I say: Mitenka!" he pronounced reproachfully, mimicking the shrill voice of the lady. "And not ashamed before folks!"

He went staggering up to the lady, who had rushed to the first chair and succeeded in making the Uhlan sit down beside her, stared at them both contemptuously and drawled in a sing-song voice—

"You're a trollop, you are, dragging your tail in the dirt!"

The lady uttered a shriek and looked about her piteously for some means of escape. She was both ashamed and frightened, and, to put the finishing touch, the officer sprang up from the chair and, with a yell, made a dash at the merchant, but, slipping, fell back into the chair with a flop. The laughter grew louder around them, and no one dreamed of helping her; but Velchaninov came to the rescue; he seized the merchant by the collar and, turning him round, thrust him five paces away from the frightened lady. And with that the scene ended; the merchant was overwhelmed by the shock and by

Velchaninov's impressive figure; his companions led him away. The dignified countenance of the elegantly dressed gentleman produced a strong effect on the jeering crowd: the laughter subsided. The lady flushed and, almost in tears, was overflowing with expressions of gratitude. The Uhlan mumbled: "Fanks, fanks!" and made as though to hold out his hand to Velchaninov, but instead of doing so suddenly took it into his head to recline at full length with his feet on the chairs.

"Mitenka!" the lady moaned reproachfully, clasping her hands in horror.

Velchaninov was pleased with the adventure and with the whole situation. The lady attracted him; she was evidently a wealthy provincial, gorgeously but tastelessly dressed, and with rather ridiculous manners—in fact, she combined all the characteristics that guarantee success to a Petersburg gallant with designs on the fair sex. A conversation sprang up; the lady bitterly complained of her husband, who "had disappeared as soon as he had got out of the carriage and so was the cause of it all, for whenever he is wanted he runs off somewhere."

"Naturally," the Uhlan muttered.

"Ah, Mitenka!" She clasped her hands again.

"Well, the husband will catch it," thought Velchaninov.

"What is his name? I will go and look for him," he suggested.

"Pal Palitch," responded the Uhlan.

"Your husband's name is Pavel Pavlovitch?" Velchaninov asked, with curiosity, and suddenly a familiar bald head was thrust between him and the lady. In a flash he had a vision of the Zahlebinins' garden, the innocent games and a tiresome bald head being incessantly thrust between him and Nadyezhda Fedosyevna.

"Here you are at last!" cried his wife hysterically.

It was Pavel Pavlovitch himself; he gazed in wonder and alarm at Velchaninov, as panic-stricken at the sight of him as though he had been a ghost. His stupefaction was such that he evidently could not for some minutes take in what his offended spouse was explaining in a rapid and irritable flow of words. At last, with a start, he grasped all the horror of his position: his own guilt, and Mitenka's behaviour, "and that this monsieur" (this was how the lady for some reason described Velchaninov) "has been a saviour and guardian angel to us, while you—you are always out of the way when you are wanted. . . ."

Velchaninov suddenly burst out laughing.

"Why, we are friends, we've been friends since childhood!" he exclaimed to the astonished lady. Putting his right arm with patronizing familiarity round the shoulders of Pavel Pavlovitch, who smiled a pale smile, "Hasn't he talked to you of Velchaninov?"

"No, he never has," the lady responded, somewhat disconcerted.

"You might introduce me to your wife, you faithless friend!"

"Lipotchka . . . it really is M. Velchaninov," Pavel Pavlovitch was beginning, but he broke off abashed.

His wife turned crimson and flashed an angry look at him, probably for the "Lipotchka."

"And, only fancy, he never let me know he was married, and never invited me to the wedding, but you, Olimpiada . . ."

"Semyonovna," Pavel Pavlovitch prompted.

"Semyonovna," the Uhlan, who had dropped asleep, echoed suddenly.

"You must forgive him, Olimpiada Semyonovna, for my sake, in honour of our meeting . . . he's a good husband."

And Velchaninov gave Pavel Pavlovitch a friendly slap on the shoulder.

"I was . . . I was only away for a minute, my love," Pavel Pavlovitch was beginning to say.

"And left your wife to be insulted," Lipotchka put in at once. "When you're wanted there's no finding you, when you're not wanted you're always at hand . . ."

"Where you're not wanted, where you're not wanted . . . where you're not wanted . . ." the Uhlan chimed in.

Lipotchka was almost breathless with excitement; she knew it was not seemly before Velchaninov, and flushed but could not restrain herself.

"Where you shouldn't be you are too attentive, too attentive!" she burst out.

"Under the bed . . . he looks for a lover under the bed—where he shouldn't . . . where he shouldn't . . ." muttered Mitenka, suddenly growing extremely excited.

But there was no doing anything with Mitenka by now. It all ended pleasantly, however, and they got upon quite friendly terms. Pavel Pavlovitch was sent to fetch coffee and soup. Olimpiada Semyonovna explained to Velchaninov that they were on their way from O——, where her husband had a post in the service, to spend two months at their country place, that it was not far off, only thirty miles from the station, that they had a lovely house and garden there, that they always had the house full of visitors, that they had neighbours too, and if Alexey Ivanovitch would be so good as to come and stay with them "in their rustic solitude" she would welcome him "as their guardian angel," for she could not recall without horror what would have happened, if . . . and so on, and so on—in fact, he was "her guardian angel. . . ."

"And saviour, and saviour," the Uhlan insisted, with heat.

Velchaninov thanked her politely, and replied that he was always at her service, that he was an absolutely idle man with no duties of any sort, and that Olimpiada Semyonovna's invitation was most flattering. He followed this at once with sprightly conversation, successfully introducing two or three compliments. Lipotchka blushed with pleasure, and as soon as Pavel Pavlovitch returned she told him enthusiastically that Alexey Ivanovitch had been so kind as to accept her invitation to spend a whole month with them in the country, and had promised to come in a week. Pavel Pavlovitch smiled in mute despair. Olimpiada Semyonovna shrugged her shoulders at him, and turned her eyes up to the ceiling. At last they got up; again a gush of gratitude, again the "guardian angel," again "Mitenka," and Pavel Pavlovitch at last escorted his wife and the Uhlan to their compartment. Velchaninov lighted a cigar and began pacing to and fro on the balcony in front of the station; he knew that Pavel Pavlovitch would run out again at once to talk to him till the bell rang. And so it happened. Pavel Pavlovitch promptly appeared before him with an uneasy expression in his face and whole figure. Velchaninov laughed, took him by the elbow in a friendly way, led him to the nearest bench, sat down himself, and made him sit down beside him. He remained silent; he wanted Pavel Pavlovitch to be the first to speak.

"So you are coming to us?" faltered the latter, going straight to the point.

"I knew that would be it! You haven't changed in the least!" laughed Velchaninov. "Why, do you mean to say"—he slapped him again on the shoulder—"do you mean to say you could seriously imagine for a moment that I could actually come and stay with you, and for a whole month too—ha-ha?"

Pavel Pavlovitch was all of a twitter.

"So you—are not coming!" he cried, not in the least disguising his relief.

"I'm not coming, I'm not coming!" Velchaninov laughed complacently.

He could not have said himself, however, why he felt so particularly amused, but he was more and more amused as time went on.

"Do you really . . . do you really mean it?"

And saying this, Pavel Pavlovitch actually jumped up from his seat in a flutter of suspense.

"Yes, I've told you already that I'm not coming, you queer fellow."

"If that's so, what am I to say to Olimpiada Semyonovna a week hence, when she will be expecting you and you don't come?"

"What a difficulty! Tell her I've broken my leg or something of that sort."

"She won't believe it," Pavel Pavlovitch drawled plaintively.

"And you'll catch it?" Velchaninov went on laughing. "But I observe, my poor friend, that you tremble before your delightful wife—don't you?"

Pavel Pavlovitch tried to smile, but it did not come off. That Velchaninov had refused to visit them was a good thing, of course, but that he should be over-familiar to him about his wife was disagreeable. Pavel Pavlovitch winced; Velchaninov noticed it. Meanwhile the second bell rang; they heard a shrill voice from the train anxiously calling Pavel Pavlovitch. The latter moved, fidgeted in his chair, but did not rise at the first summons, evidently expecting something more from Velchaninov, no doubt another assurance that he would not come and stay with them.

"What was your wife's maiden name?" Velchaninov inquired, as though unaware of Pavel Pavlovitch's anxiety.

"She is our priest's daughter," replied the latter in uneasy trepidation, listening and looking towards the train.

"Ah, I understand, you married her for her beauty."

Pavel Pavlovitch winced again.

"And who's this Mitenka with you?"

"Oh, he's a distant relation of ours—that is, of mine; the son of my deceased cousin. His name's Golubtchikov, he was degraded for disorderly behaviour in the army, but now he has been promoted again and we have been getting his equipment. . . . He's an unfortunate young man. . . ."

"To be sure, the regular thing; the party's complete," thought Velchaninov.

"Pavel Pavlovitch!" the call came again from the train, and by now with a marked tone of irritation in the voice.

"Pal Palitch!" they heard in another thick voice.

Pavel Pavlovitch fidgeted and moved restlessly again, but Velchaninov took him by the elbow and detained him.

"How would you like me to go this minute and tell your wife how you tried to cut my throat?"

"What, what!" Pavel Pavlovitch was terribly alarmed. "God forbid!"

"Pavel Pavlovitch! Pavel Pavlovitch!" voices were heard calling again.

"Well, be off now!" said Velchaninov, letting him go at last, and still laughing genially.

"So you won't come?" Pavel Pavlovitch whispered for the last time, almost in despair, and even put his hands before him with the palms together in his old style.

"Why, I swear I won't come! Run, there'll be trouble, you know."

And with a flourish he held out his hand to him—and was startled at the result: Pavel Pavlovitch did not take his hand, he even drew his own hand back.

The third bell rang.

In one instant something strange happened to both of them: both seemed transformed. Something, as it were, quivered and burst out in Velchaninov, who had been laughing only just before. He clutched Pavel Pavlovitch by the shoulder and held him in a tight and furious grip.

"If I—I hold out this hand to you," showing the palm of his left hand, where a big scar from the cut was still distinct, "you certainly might take it!" he whispered, with pale and trembling lips.

Pavel Pavlovitch, too, turned pale, and his lips trembled too; a convulsive quiver ran over his face.

"And Liza?" he murmured in a rapid whisper, and suddenly his lips, his cheeks and his chin began to twitch and tears gushed from his eyes.

Velchaninov stood before him stupefied.

"Pavel Pavlovitch! Pavel Pavlovitch!" they heard a scream from the train as though some one were being murdered—and suddenly the whistle sounded.

Pavel Pavlovitch roused himself, flung up his hands and ran full speed to the train; the train was already in motion, but he managed to hang on somehow, and went flying to his compartment. Velchaninov remained at the station and only in the evening set off on his original route in another train. He did not turn off to the right to see his fair friend—he felt too much out of humour. And how he regretted it afterwards!